T0248172

1860

America Moves Toward War

Michael J. Deeb

1860

America Moves Toward War

Addison & Highsmith

Addison & Highsmith Publishers

Las Vegas ◊ Chicago ◊ Palm Beach

Published in the United States of America by
Histria Books
7181 N. Hualapai Way, Ste. 130-86
Las Vegas, NV 89166 USA
HistriaBooks.com

Addison & Highsmith is an imprint of Histria Books. Titles published under the imprints of Histria Books are distributed worldwide.

Library of Congress Control Number: 2023937875

ISBN 978-1-59211-308-8 (hardcover)
ISBN 978-1-59211-327-9 (eBook)

My thanks go to my teachers, Sister Roberta,
Sister Noella, and in particular, Mr. Lewis Clingman.

Introduction

The male voters in the United States were about to elect the sixteenth president in the nation's history. Many feared that this November 1860 election might prove to be the last the voters would cast as citizens in the thirty-three states that made up the United States of America.

The students attending the Lowell, Michigan, primary school discussed the issues of that day; the upcoming presidential election, slavery, secession, and the war which might follow. Such matters were also of concern to their parents at home.

This story will explore the concerns of young and old alike in that Michigan community, their effort to understand the issues at stake in 1860, and their reaction to the possible break-up of the Union.

United States of America: 1860

The Fishing Hole

Located on a tract of land near the Drieborg farm was a good-sized pond. Some would call it a lake. During the hot summer, members of the nearby families would use it to cool off with a swim or maybe use poles and hooks to catch fish.

Michael Drieborg and his teenage friends, Willie Turbush and Ethan Schock would meet there to fish and talk whenever they could get away from farm chores and weren't in school.

Today, they sought relief from harvesting corn on their parents' farms. Every farm in the Lowell, Michigan, area grew that crop, and it was time for the fall harvest. School was closed, so the boys and girls could help out at home. By Friday noon, most of the fields had been cleared, and the corn cribs filled.

So, their parents had given the boys the afternoon off. They headed to the pond. In late October, it was too chilly to swim but still perfect for fishing.

Willie and Ethan were already sitting on the bank with their fishing lines in the water.

"What do you think is keeping Drieborg?" Willie wondered aloud.

"Who knows?" Ethan responded. "His papa is a tough one if you ask me. He probably had one more chore for Mike."

It wasn't long before they heard someone coming through the woods surrounding the pond. It was the missing teenager of their group, Michael Drieborg.

"Good thing you weren't trying to sneak up on us, Drieborg. I could hear you coming a mile away," Willie said, making fun of his friend.

Ethan joined in the fun. "All that noise you were making, no wonder we haven't gotten any bites. The fish could hear you tramping through the wood, for sure."

"That's very funny, you two," Michael responded. "How many times have we fished here this year? And how many keepers have either of you caught? I'll tell you how many. I can count them on the fingers of one hand. That's how many. So, don't give me that guff about noise."

Mike nudged Willie. "Move over, Turbush. Give me some room here."

"What are you using for bait today, Ethan?"

"What else? Worms, of course."

"I brought along some stale bread my momma was going to give to the pigs. Want to try some of that for bait?"

"Who ever heard of using bread?" Willie exclaimed. "Fish in this pond are partial to worms. You can keep your stale bread."

"All right, you two," Michael said, "tell you what. Whoever catches the most keepers gets all the fish to take home. It will be my bread against your worms. How about it; is it a bet?"

"No contest, Drieborg. Kiss your catch goodbye. Right, Ethan?"

The boys were silent for a while. Each one was hoping to be the first to catch a keeper.

"Hey, you guys," Willie suddenly asked, "are you two going to join up when the war starts?"

"What war?" Drieborg asked.

"You must have been absent from school when Clingman told us about the war, Mike."

"Will you tell me what war you're talking about?"

"He said he has been getting letters from relatives down south saying that if Lincoln is elected, a whole bunch of the cotton states will leave the Union. Then there will be a war."

Michael still had questions. "Did he say why there would be a war?"

"He didn't get into that much except that his relatives figured Lincoln would try to stop those states from leaving the Union by using force. That's why he said there would be a war."

"I'd join up in a minute," Ethan said. "Anything to get off the farm; 'sides, it would be great fun."

"You could get killed, Schock," Mike warned him.

"Are you scared, Mike?" Willie taunted.

"Maybe I am," Mike snapped back. "Just seems to me that war means battles, and battles mean killing. I don't see much fun in that. Besides, why does anyone care if the Slave States leave the Union?"

Schock answered. "Now that you mention it, Mike, I don't rightly know."

Willie added, "Must be pretty important though if our teacher, Mr. Clingman, says there'll be a war. He's a pretty smart guy."

"Hey! I got a bite!" Willie shouted, pulling up on his pole. Sure enough, he had. The boys saw a good-sized fish break the surface of the lake attached to his line by a hook.

"How about that, Drieborg?" he bragged. "My worm did the trick."

Ethan laughed, too. "Want to use some of my worms, Mike?"

"I don't see you catching any keepers, Ethan," Mike taunted.

Then the boys settled down to some serious fishing.

Ethan Schock was the first to break the silence.

"Hey, Mike. How'd you like it when you were with Louise in the barn?"

"That's sort of private, don't you think?"

Willie laughed out loud. "Crying out loud, Drieborg, don't be so touchy. Ethan and I have been with her, too. In fact, every one of the boys at school older than your twelve-year-old brother Jacob has been to the barn with Louise. And it's never a secret, either. 'Cause afterward, Louise brags about it to all the girls at school. I'm sure she told your sisters. Even my sister knows about you spending some time with Louise."

"Oh my gosh!" Mike exclaimed. "If either of my sisters ever tells my parents, I'm in real trouble."

Willie had two older sisters still at home. "If I know sisters, Mike. And oh, yes, do I know sisters. They'll wait for just the right moment to tell your parents how evil their little son is. They might do it to get even for something you said or because you wouldn't do something they asked of you. Or maybe it's just that time of the month when girls seem most irritable. Just you wait, Mike. But you can count on it. One of them will tell."

Mike fell back on the grass. "You sure know how to ruin a guy's afternoon, Willie," Mike moaned. "What happened to you when your father found out?"

"Out in our barn, he took a strap to me. All the while he was whipping me, he told me how stupid I had been. Believe me, outside the classroom, I haven't been within a mile of Louise or her barn since. And I won't be, either."

"What an afternoon this has turned out to be," Mike complained. "The fish are ignoring my stale bread bait. Ethan tells me our country will be at war soon, and Willie tells me I'm probably going to get a whipping from my father for going to the barn with Louise. Thanks a lot, you two."

Willie wasn't finished funnin' with his friend. "It could be worse, Mike."

"How could it be worse?"

"There could be a war, and you joined the army."

"I suppose that could be worse," Mike agreed.

Ethan jumped into the kidding around and said, "There's something a lot worse than that."

"What could be worse than going off to fight in a war?" Willie asked.

"One of us would have to marry Louise. That's what."

"Oh my gosh!" Mike exclaimed in alarm, "that would be worse."

No one spoke after that. Mike even ignored the fish pulling at the bait on his hook.

Lowell, Michigan

It was a beautiful October day in Michigan. The sun was up, and the color of the leaves on the maple and oak trees had begun to change from summer green to the gold and reds of fall. It would be a fine day for squirrel hunting. But the two teenage Drieborg boys were not in the woods. Instead, they were cleaning the family barn of animal droppings.

Mike, the eldest of the Drieborg children at seventeen, was at least six feet tall. His twelve-year-old brother Jacob couldn't quite look his older brother in the eye, but he was catching up rapidly. Their Dutch heritage was evident in their blond hair, blue eyes, and fair skin. They looked remarkably like their papa, Jake. And, like most farm boys, they had chores. Every day they had chores to do. Today, it was cleaning the barn.

"Do animals really care if the barn floor is clean of poop and covered with fresh hay?"

"That has nothing to do with it," Michael told his younger brother. "We're Dutch, remember. And the Dutch will have a barn that is clean as a whistle."

"What does that mean, anyway, Michael, 'clean as a whistle'?" Jacob asked.

"It means that we had better have this place cleaned up before Papa gets home. That's what."

"Why can't I ever go to town on Saturday morning with papa?" the twelve-year-old Jacob complained.

Mike chuckled. "Because you are not yet thirteen, Jacob; you know the family rule. Next year you can take a turn with us. Not till then."

"It's a dumb rule, if you ask me."

"Nobody asked you, little brother." Michael was a loving brother, but he loved to kid Jacob.

"You know, Mike," Jacob snapped back. "I'm not so little anymore." Actually, Jacob *could* look his over-six-foot-tall brother in the eyes.

"That's true, Jacob. Sorry," Mike responded, suddenly aware that he had hurt his brother's feelings. "I'll try to remember that."

Jacob wasn't finished sharing the complaints of the youngest in the family.

"And why do we boys have to shovel out the manure from the barn stalls and empty the pots in the water closet every morning and night? Why can't the girls do some of this stuff?"

"You got me on that one, for sure, Jacob. I suppose it's as simple as this. The momma and girls take care of the house, the chickens, and the garden and do all the cooking. The papa and the boys take care of planting, harvesting, milking cows, chopping wood, slaughtering pigs, cleaning up the manure in the barn, and all the other dirty jobs on a farm."

Jacob lifted the handles on the wheelbarrow. But before he pushed it toward the manure pit, he declared, "That does it. I've decided, Michael. You're lookin' at one fella who's not going ta do this the rest of his life. No sir! As soon as I can, I'm off."

"I suppose you will, Jacob. But, for now, I suggest you get a move on. Papa left for town early this morning. You don't want to be around if he gets back before we finish."

"I know, Mike. I'm moving."

In Town

Their father, Jake Drieborg, and their sister, Ann, had gone to the village of Lowell, located a few miles from his farm. It was a community of fewer than two hundred residents. They were shopkeepers, skilled tradesmen, and professionals who catered to the needs of the surrounding farming population. Buildings were located on either side of Main Street, a dirt road that ran east and west. The Flat River ran north and south through the center of town.

In 1860 Lowell had the Franklin House Hotel, White's Boot and Shoe shop, Mr. Vanderburgh's drugstore, the Daniels and Young grocery, along with Zania's general store, and Joe Seville's Empire Saloon. Miss Carpenter operated a dressmaking shop, and Mr. Blasdell owned a hardware store. John Blain and Steve Denny were the local blacksmiths, while John Chapman was the town marshal. Jacob Snell and Joseph Deeb were the attorneys in town, with Deeb serving as Justice of the Peace. Dr. A. Peck was the only licensed medical doctor and had a dentist working with him, Dr. Perry. Mr. Harvey Bacon owned the Lowell Bank, and every farmer and businessman seemed to owe his bank money. Mr. Spefford was the owner and publisher of a weekly newspaper launched in September 1860.

Today, Jake had some of his wheat crop with him. He needed it ground into flour at the Hatch and Craw grain elevator. He also had to buy a list of things from Zania's general store for his wife, Rose.

Earlier than usual today, he had finished his farm chores so he could be in town when the stores and the grain elevator opened at seven. And, even though he didn't want to spend the time before he left, he cleaned up and changed his clothing before his departure, leaving his smelly work clothes at home.

"Seems like there are always farmers waiting with their wagons at the elevator; maybe today the line won't be so long if I get there early enough," he thought.

Just in case he was wrong, Jake sent his daughter, Ann, to the general store with her mother's order while he went to the elevator. Sure enough, despite his early arrival, he still found several other farmers with their wagons ahead of him.

At Zania's general store, Ann had to wait her turn, too.

"I'll be with you shortly, Ann," Mr. Zania's wife, Mable, told her. "I've got just two more orders to fill before I get to yours."

"Thank you, Mrs. Zania," Ann responded respectfully. "Can I look through the latest catalog while I'm waiting?"

"Sure enough, Ann. You can find it on that counter to the left of the door."

As soon as she opened the thick catalog, Ann went straight to the dress patterns. The Fall Harvest Dance was coming up at the school. She wanted something special to wear.

"Maybe something blue would go well with my light brown hair and blue eyes," she thought.

A pretty girl with a bright smile, Ann was looking forward to the dance this year. Since she was now thirteen, her parents would allow her to dance with a boy for the first time. She knew she would find one tall enough to dance with her. She was certain of that.

"Your momma's order is ready, Ann," she heard Mrs. Zania shout from the counter. "You want my delivery boy, Ethan, to carry the box to your wagon?"

"Yes, please," Ann answered.

"How about I include a copy of the catalog you're looking at?"

"Thank you, Mrs. Zania. That is most kind of you."

"If you and Susan want new dresses for the Harvest Dance, you had better get your order for the patterns and cloth into me soon."

"Would next Saturday be too late, Mrs. Zania?" Ann asked.

"No, that would be fine. By the way, tell your mother I have added the cost of your order to your bill."

Ethan Schock placed the box containing her mother's order by the front door. He was her brother Michael's age, seventeen. Ethan wasn't as tall as Mike, but tall enough for her purpose.

"Hello, Ethan," she said. "How long have you worked here?"

"This is my second Saturday. Didn't you see me last week, Ann?"

"No. We didn't come to town last Saturday. How is it that your father doesn't need you on the farm?"

"We have a hired hand now, a cousin from Prussia. So I can work here one day a week."

Ann wasn't finished planting a seed with Ethan, "Will you be going to the Harvest Dance?"

"I suppose so. Are you?"

"Yes, I am. Maybe I'll save you a dance."

Just then, her father walked up to the two teenagers. "Is the order ready, Ann?"

"Yes, it is, Papa. You know Ethan Schock?"

"No, I've not met him." Jake extended his hand to the boy, "But I just spoke with his papa Carl at da elevator. Good morning, Ethan."

"Good morning, Mr. Drieborg. You want me to carry your order to the wagon, sir?"

"No thanks, son. I'll get it. Come, Ann. We must go."

"Bye, Ethan," Ann said.

"I'll see you in school, Ann," he responded.

***

Jake's wife, Rose, was home today. Usually, she was with her husband on these Saturday morning trips. She enjoyed hearing the latest news from the other ladies she met at the general store. But today, she had work to do at home that just couldn't wait.

She was in the house with her fifteen-year-old daughter, Susan, who was helping her mother, can chicken. Susan was shorter than her sister Ann. She had blond hair and fair skin. Her ready smile and cheerful disposition had made it easy for her to attract boys as dance partners during last year's Harvest Dance.

***

Back in Lowell, it was almost nine o'clock. Jake's flour was sacked and loaded in the back of the wagon, along with his wife's order from the general store. He was eager to get home; he had work to do there today, too.

Before they left town, though, Jake told Ann he was worried.

"You're sure you got everything on your mother's list, Ann? I don't want to get home and find we have forgotten something. If we did, we'd hear about it from your momma until we got back to town next Saturday."

"Yes, Papa," Ann insisted, "I understand. I still have the list in my pocket. Do you want to stop the wagon so I can unpack the box from the general store? Then you can check each item. For heaven's sake, Papa, don't you trust me?" Ann was a very pretty brunette, almost five-feet-six inches tall. Bright and serious, she did not put up with foolish questions, even from her father.

"Yes, yes, I trust you, Ann," Jake assured her. "I just don't want your momma after me all week if we forgot something."

"I don't either, Papa," Ann agreed. "I double-checked the order before you loaded it on the wagon."

The Drieborg wagon was now outside Lowell, headed west on Fulton Street. Jake and his daughter would be home in less than an hour. "Papa," Ann said, "did you see the man who was unloading those boxes at Mr. Zania's store?"

"Yes, daughter, I did."

"He's a Negro, isn't he?"

"How do you know dat, Ann?" She sometimes surprised him with her questions. But he admired her inquiring nature.

"I learned about them at school, Papa. Mr. Clingman, our teacher, showed us pictures of slaves. They all looked like the man I saw today. Do you think that the Negro man I saw is a slave?"

"No, Ann. He's no slave. At da elevator today, I heard dat da Negro man you saw works for Mr. Thompson's freight company. I heard dat he was a slave, but he escaped and arrived in Grand Rapids a few weeks ago."

"He probably came on the underground railroad, Papa. Mr. Clingman said that Negroes who have escaped were once owned by somebody. He said that our Marshal Chapman is supposed to arrest the runaways so they can be returned to their owner. Is that true, Papa?"

"Yes, it is, Ann. In da South, Negro people are considered property. Dey is called slaves. Dey are bought and sold just like we would buy horses or cows. Slaves must do whatever da owner demands, too. Even da children become slaves when dey is born. Da owner can break up slave families and sell da parents or even da children if dey wish."

"How terrible, Papa. And this is allowed in our country?"

"Yes, it is. Ask your teacher, Ann. He will tell you dat it has been allowed in da United States for over two hundred years already."

The two were silent for a while.

Ann broke the silence. "Do we have slaves in Michigan, Papa?"

"No, Ann. Slaves are only found in da South, mainly where dey grow cotton. But slave owners want to be able to take slaves everywhere in da United States, Even to Michigan. Mr. Lincoln's Republican Party opposes da spread of slavery. I read dat da argument about where slavery will be allowed is a big part of da election for president dat is coming in November."

"Well, then, I hope Mr. Lincoln wins. Don't you, Papa?"

"I am thinking of voting for him in November, Ann."

"How do you know so much about this, Papa?"

"Your momma and me, we read da Grand Rapids Eagle newspaper. Der are stories all da time about da coming election and what da candidates are saying about important things like slavery.

"Momma likes Mr. Lincoln, too."

"But Momma can't vote, can she, Papa?"

"No, Ann. Women can't vote in da United States."

"That is so wrong, Papa."

"Maybe so, Ann. But even men like me had no vote in da old country or anywhere else in da world for dat matter. Only in da United States can ordinary people like me vote. Women's time will probably come. Just now is not da time."

"It can't come too soon to suit me, Papa."

"When it does, I'm sure you will be da first person at da voting place on Election Day."

"You can count on that, Papa."

***

Rose Drieborg and Susan were finishing up with the chicken canning at home. The last of the jars were sealed and in the boiling water.

"Momma, this is only the second time I remember you canning chicken. What did you and Papa do before that?"

"Before we started canning things last year, we dried fruit and stored it in the cellar and cured chickens in the smokehouse. We had potatoes, carrots, and onions most of the winter, but we had to do without other vegetables and fruit or buy them packed in tin cans."

"Two years ago, though, the Zanias brought a man to our church. And, after Mass one Sunday, he gave some of us a demonstration of a new food preservation process called canning. It was invented in 1858 by a man named Mason. Using his special lids to seal the bottles, food of all sorts can be stored for rather long periods of time. So, your papa and I decided to try it."

"Papa is so set in his ways. I'm surprised that he would allow even trying such a new method."

"You don't know your papa as well as you think you do, Susan. He is a stubborn Dutchman who is comfortable with things being done the way they have always been done. I'll grant you that. But he is always looking for ways to improve the farm and our lives. He saw this canning process as a way of making better use of the food we produce. He agreed with me that if this process worked, we would eat better, too. So we tried it, and I believe it has helped us a lot."

"It sure has, Momma," Susan agreed. "We still haven't opened all the jars in the cellar. I'll bet we'll have a hard time using all the fruit and vegetables you canned this summer before next year's harvest."

"Maybe you're right, daughter. But it is nice to have that problem rather than having too few jars full or none at all."

But now Rose and her daughter had to clean up the mess.

"Phew!" Rose said as she wiped the perspiration from her brow on her apron. "This was a good job done today, Susan. We should have just enough time now to clean up and fix dinner."

"Some people in town call the noon meal lunch and the evening meal dinner. Why don't we, Momma?"

"I can't explain what other people do, daughter. All I know is that since your papa and I have been in this country, we have called the noon meal dinner. Maybe it is because we still have so much work yet to do in the afternoon that we need the energy we get from a big meal. Our work is over by the evening, so we have a lighter meal and call it supper. Does that make sense?"

"Yes, it does, Momma," Susan agreed. "What are we having for dinner today?"

"What else? We'll have chicken."

"Ugh! After killing and skinning so many of them this morning, I don't think I will ever be able to look at another chicken without gagging."

"You'll get over it, sweetheart. Just because you peeled the apples last night, does that mean you don't want to eat any of the apple pie you fixed this morning?"

"Oh, Momma! That's funny. Of course, I'll want a piece of pie."

"Well, you best get a move on, young lady. As soon as we clean up the kitchen, you have to peel the potatoes. I'll fry the chicken. Does that sound like a good plan?"

"Fine, Momma," Susan responded. "I must say, when Ann went to town with Papa this morning, she missed all the hard work of canning."

"It was her turn to go with Papa today," Rose reminded her daughter.

"It just seems that she always manages to get out of the dirty work. Like, when we're hoeing the garden, I've seen her leaning on her hoe, daydreaming most of the time."

"If you were watching your sister, you must not have been hoeing either, eh? Come, you take care of Susan. Ann is my concern, not yours."

"Oh, all right, Momma."

Home

Jake and Ann were in front of their home before they knew it. Jake used the reins to direct the horse off the road and into the barnyard behind the house. The dwelling was built some thirty yards north of Fulton Street. There, the Drieborgs owned 180 acres, a typical-sized farm for that day. Ninety of those acres were south of Fulton Street and stretched all the way to the Grand River. There was a large stand of trees north of the house as well. Handy for firewood.

The Drieborg home was constructed of wood. Most of the house sat on a stone foundation and over what was referred to as a Michigan basement. This space was also called a storm cellar. It had a dirt floor and was the room where vegetables from the family garden were stored. It had a low ceiling, so Jake and his son Michael, who were both over six feet tall, had to stoop when they moved around under the house.

The main room above had a front door in the center and opened onto a porch facing Fulton Street. A window was to the right and a fireplace to the left. This fireplace was where Rose did the cooking and baked her bread and pies. She and her husband had a bedroom at one end of the house, and the two girls had one at the other end. The two boys slept in a loft above the girls' bedroom.

Jake had designed his home carefully. He arranged for cooking water to be drawn inside the house by placing a hand pump on the kitchen sink. Using that pump, water could be pulled into the house from the well outside.

Many farmers used rainwater for personal use. They channeled rain from the house roof down a pipe into a barrel in the cellar, where it was stored until needed for cooking and washing. Others filled buckets with water at their outdoor pump and carried them into the house from there, not a pleasant chore in the winter.

Jake also enclosed the back porch. There, everyone hung up their coats and changed their work boots for house shoes before entering the main house. This rear entrance also had a stairway to the cellar on one side and a water closet on the other. Much to the disgust of his two sons, the job of emptying the chamber pots in this closet each day fell to them.

The barn sat some twenty yards to the north of the house. There were stalls for two milking cows and another for the plow horse. A fourth stall was currently empty. There were double doors at each end of the building. The double doors at the east end opened into a series of pens for the pigs, sheep, goats, and cattle. Hay was stored in the barn loft, where it could be easily dropped into the stalls for the animals. At the other end of the loft was a good-sized room for their farmhand whenever they had one.

A corn crib, a smokehouse, and a chicken coop rounded out the buildings. Along with the manure pit, they were all sufficiently distant to keep the smells and smoke away from the house. Down by the river and farthest away from the house was the ice house. It was filled with ice cut from the river during the winter. In the summer, the family enjoyed the luxury of ice, sometimes even late into the fall.

All in all, the Drieborg place was well designed. Jacob and Rose were additionally fortunate to have four healthy children to help run the farm. Their teenage complaints aside, the children understood their roles and accepted them.

Dinner Time

No sooner had Jake stopped the wagon in his barnyard than he was giving orders.

"Jacob," he began, "give Ann a hand with da groceries. Take dem right into da house. Momma will tell you what to do with dem."

"Yes, Papa," Jacob responded.

"Michael, you take da wagon into da barn, unhitch da horse, and feed her, too."

"Yes, Papa," Mike responded.

"I'll take da flour sack into da house. It would be a terrible mess if one of you boys dropped it."

As he picked up the flour and headed inside the house, Jake said to no one in particular, "You boys finish cleaning da barn? I hope so. We got a lot of other work to do dis afternoon, too."

Mike chuckled to himself. "*I knew he would say that. Some things never change,*" he thought to himself.

When Mike was feeding the horse, his brother Jacob walked into the barn. Jake was right behind him, looking over the cleaning job they had done in the barn.

"Not bad, boys," he said. "You done a good job, seems to me. Now, we get all da harness gear down from da hooks. Hang 'em over da sides of da stalls. We're gonna give each one a good oiling. Look for tears and weak spots. Den, we can see which ones need repair, too."

They began to work on the leather gear.

Jake asked his eldest son, "Do you know da Ethan Schock boy, Michael?"

"Sure, Papa," Mike responded. "I sit next to him in school, and he and I fish and hunt together sometimes, too."

"Is he a trustworthy sort of boy?"

"You mean would I trust him to walk Ann home from school or to dance with her at the Harvest Dance?"

"How do you know I'm asking about dat?"

"Well, Papa," Michael responded with a big smile. "It's not hard for me to figure out. You went into town this morning, and Ann went with you. Ethan is working at Zania's general store as a delivery boy. He also carries groceries for customers and loads the packages on their wagons. Ann probably went to the store to fill Momma's order while you were at the elevator. I would guess that Ethan carried Ann's order to the loading dock, and they had a conversation. Sort of normal, I'd say. What are you worried about, Papa?"

"Nothing, really. I just wondered."

"I wouldn't worry about Ann, Papa," Mike told him. "I've seen her handle boys at school. They don't hassle her. Believe me, she is one tough customer."

They were only half done with the harnesses when Ann entered the barn.

"Momma says it's almost time for dinner."

Immediately, Jake stopped what he was doing and stood. "Get washed up, boys," he told his sons. "You know how your momma gets if we are late for one of her meals."

***

The family was seated around the table.

"Michael," his mother said. "Please say the prayer."

"Come, Lord Jesus, be our guest.

And to our bodies, may this food be blessed.

May we show our gratitude by helping others who are in need.

Amen."

"Thank you, son."

"Now, Papa," she continued. "Please begin passing the plates of food. Start with the chicken, if you would."

"Yes, Momma."

"It all smells good, Momma," Jacob told her.

Ann chuckled, "There is never food on the table that doesn't appeal to you, little brother. You're always hungry."

"That's right. I am always hungry. What's it to you?"

"Say only nice things, you two. I won't have squabbling at my table. Pass the potatoes, Susan."

"Yes, Momma."

Once everyone had filled their plates, Rose asked,

"What is the news from town?"

Ann spoke first. "Mrs. Zania said that if we had our orders to her next Saturday, she could get our dress patterns and cloth in plenty of time for us to make dresses for the Harvest Dance. She sent a catalog for us to look over, too, Momma."

"I saw it in the box. Did you get a chance to look at patterns while you were waiting for your papa?"

"Yes, I did," Ann responded. "I saw a nice pattern. And, sky blue cloth would make a beautiful dress with it."

"After dinner, we will look them over. You look too, Susan. We need one for you as well."

"Ann was talking with Ethan Schock at the general store," Jake told everyone.

Ann blushed some. "I just thanked him for carrying our order out for me. That's all, Momma."

"That's all right, Ann," Her mother assured her. "Papa and I know the Schock family. They are very nice people and good farmers, too."

"I think dey are Lutherans, Momma," Jake said.

Susan joined the conversation. "What has that got to do with anything, Papa?"

Her father responded. "Drieborgs are Catholic, Susan. You and Ann are almost women now. Soon you both will be thinking about marriage and a family of your own. When dat time comes, you must marry a Catholic. So, it is not good for you to get too friendly with boys who are Protestants."

"Can't we even talk to boys like Ethan?" Ann asked.

"Certainly, you can," their mother assured them. "Just remember that soon boys will be asking if they can call on you. We will only allow boys from Catholic families to court you. Just so you know, girls."

"Oh, Momma!" Susan sighed.

Ann piped up. "What about Michael and Louise Mohr? Does the same apply to him?"

Rose Drieborg asked. "What about the Mohr girl, Michael?"

"We're just school friends, Momma."

Ann wasn't done, though. "What school lessons did she teach you when you two were in her barn loft, Michael?" Both she and her sister Susan covered their smiles and quiet laughter with their dinner napkins.

Jake Drieborg entered the conversation again. "Michael," he said quite firmly. "Da same warning goes for you, son. You will marry a Catholic girl. You must not be meeting dis Mohr girl any place but school. After we finish in da barn dis afternoon, I think you and I will have a talk about dis friendship of yours."

"Yes, Papa," Mike responded glumly. "Thanks a lot, Ann," He whispered to her.

She whispered back, "What's good for the goose is good for the gander, brother."

"That big mouth Ann sure got me in trouble," Mike thought.

Susan served everyone a piece of pie while Ann refilled the glasses with milk.

"What else is there from town, Papa?" Rose asked her husband.

"Ann saw a Negro man who works for Johnson's freight company unloading a wagon at Mr. Zania's store."

Excited, Ann began. "You should have seen him. He was big like you, Michael. And he looked just like the pictures of Negro slaves Mr. Clingman showed us at school. The man had skin that was almost black, and his hair was short and curly."

Jacob, who was sometimes called Little Jake, groused. "I miss all the good stuff."

"Did you talk with him, Ann?" Susan asked.

"Oh, no," she responded quickly. "I was too surprised just seeing him in the store. I looked up, and there he was, right next to me, almost. He was so big and dark. I must admit he frightened me."

"Papa told me later that he heard this Negro man had been a slave and had run away from somewhere in the South."

Mike spoke up. "I wonder if he came north on the Underground Railroad Mr. Clingman told us about? When we get back to school next week, Ann, you have to be sure to tell him about what you saw in town today."

"Can you imagine being owned by someone else, like that man was?" Susan asked.

"It was almost like dat in Holland, children," their father said.

Jake had told Mike stories about the old country when they were alone in the barn together, milking cows. Mike had heard his father speak of this before. But his sisters and brother had not.

"Tell us, Papa. Were you really slaves?" Little Jake asked.

"Before I answer dat, son," Jake began, "let me explain about land in da old country. Since da time of da Roman Empire even, land in da European countries was owned by very few people. Rulers controlled da land and gave some of it to men loyal to dem, who helped make the ruler strong with der soldiers. Dey were called by many different titles, but dey were da lord of da manor or castle and owner of da land. For hundreds of years, people like my papa and momma worked da land for such men. People who worked da land were called serfs in some places or yeomen in other places. In all places, dey were under da strict control of da lord.

"After each harvest, da crops belonged to da lord. People like my papa were only allowed to keep a small amount of it. Dat could be a very small amount in a bad year. If da papa was sick, he could end up owing da lord more crops dan he had been able to grow. Den, even da children might be taken away to work somewhere else just to pay da debt. And da serfs were not allowed to leave da land where dey was born. Dey was tied to da land for all der lives.

"So, children, da situation der is very much like da slavery we have in our country."

"We learned about that in history class, Papa," Michael told everyone, "it was called the feudal system. Serfs were also called peasants. They were virtually owned by the lord and had to do exactly as he demanded."

"Is that why you came to this country, Papa?" Ann asked.

"Dat is why, daughter. My papa was a hard worker and loyal to his lord. But he wanted me to have a better life. When I was very young, der was a war. My older brother had been taken by our lord to serve in his army. We never heard from my brother again. So, when papa heard dat another war was starting, my father was worried for me.

"Prussia was having a war with another German state, and Holland had been drawn into it. My parents did not want me to be taken like my brother, so dey used some money dey had hidden, and with some help from my uncle, who was in America, dey snuck me away one night and got me on a ship to dis country."

"What about you, Momma?" Susan asked. "Was it better for girls there?"

"No, it wasn't," Rose responded. "In fact, I think it was worse. Girls had to work in the fields just as hard as the men. And, after we were given to some man in marriage, we had to bear children as well as work. Besides that, during all the wars, when soldiers came through, they would treat women badly, kill the little children and maybe take the older ones.

"My family originally lived in France. In fact, our name was Franz. But, the government in our part of that country persecuted Catholics. They killed our priests and drove the Catholic families off the land. So, my family had to find another place to live. They went to the Catholic part of Holland.

"My papa was a blacksmith. So he had no trouble finding work there. After my momma died, though, he took me, my brother Aaron and my sister Margaret on a boat headed for America. My papa died on the journey, so Aaron, Margaret, and I arrived here alone. We had relatives in this part of Michigan. So, we came to this area. I met your papa at our church."

"We've been to Aunt Margaret's house in Sparta, Momma. Whatever happened to Uncle Aaron?" Michael asked. "It has been so long since I've seen him that I can't even remember what he looked like."

"You were only a baby when he last visited us, Michael. Susan wasn't even born yet. Some time ago, he wrote me that he was in the timber country of northern Michigan. He might still be there for all I know. He always kept to himself when we were youngsters. He probably still does."

"Dat's enough," Jake told everyone. "Come boys, we have work to finish in da barn, eh."

The Facts of Life

Jake and his sons were soon out in the barn oiling all the leather gear used with their horse. Such devices were called tack and harnessed their only horse to either their wagon or their plow. Any frayed leather they found was set aside for repair or replacement. Jake would decide afterward.

This was also a time for Jake to teach his sons about the care and repair of tack that was essential to every farmer. Finished with that, he would remind them about caring for their plow horse.

"Every day, you must examine our horse for sores. When you are giving him his daily brushing is a good time to look for dem. Pay good attention around da head. If you find a sore spot or a cut, put ointment on it, and show it to me. If it is bad enough, I might decide we need to rest him for a day or two till da problem clears up."

"Seems like a lot 'a fuss over an ol' horse, Papa," Little Jake grumbled.

"Would you rather pull da wagon or have our horse do it, son?"

"I sure don't want to pull no wagon or plow either," Little Jake responded.

"Dat's why we must take such good care of Blue. Do you understand now, son?"

"Yes, Papa."

Jake showed his sons what he meant. As he brushed the horse, he ran his hands over the coat. Today, he did not find any cuts or sore spots. "Dat is how I want you to do it. You understand, boys?"

In unison, they answered, "Yes, Papa."

Mike thought, *"I know Papa thinks this is important. But gosh, this is probably the tenth time he has gone over this with me."*

Jake moved on to the other matter that was on his mind.

"Michael," he began. "Tell me about your friendship with dis Mohr girl."

"Can't you send Jacob to the house or something, Papa?" Michael whined. "I would prefer to have this conversation with you alone."

"I don't think so, Michael," Jake said. "I think it good for Jacob to hear dis conversation. So, you answer my question about da Mohr girl; Jacob will listen."

"Oh, all right, Papa."

"Louise and I met a couple of times in her barn alone," Mike began.

"What did you and Louise do when you met alone in her family's barn?"

Mike paused and reddened.

"Yes, Michael?" his father prodded.

Finally, his seventeen-year-old son said, "We kissed, Papa."

"Did you touch da girl anyplace else?"

Another long pause prompted Jake to prod his son again.

"Would you rather have we had dis conversation in da house with Momma and your sisters listening, Michael?"

"Oh! No Papa. Please."

"Well, den. Answer my question. You were in da hay loft with da girl, I suppose?"

"Yes, we were." Mike choked on the words.

"I can hardly stand to answer. Papa knows everything! And Jacob is sitting right there, listening; I hate this."

"Do you like dis girl a lot, Michael?" his father continued. "Is she beautiful?"

Little Jake interrupted. "I'd say she was downright ugly, Papa."

"I'm asking Michael, son. You just listen."

"Michael?"

"She's pretty plain, Papa."

"You boys know how our farm animals mate. Den, we get a few more ducks, some piglets, and maybe a lamb. If we are lucky, we get anoder cow, even. God designed dis all. He also made women to bear children and men to sire dem.

"Did you do anything dat could have brought a child into da world, son?"

"No! I didn't do that, Papa." Michael almost shouted. "I wouldn't do that until I was married."

"You do realize dat you could have made a baby had you done dat?"

"Yes, I know, Papa." Michael insisted. "But I didn't go that far."

"But you went to dis barn when you knew what dis girl wanted of you. Am I right, son?"

"Yes, Papa."

"Remember how Eve led Adam to eat da fruit of da forbidden tree? You see how dat got dem thrown out of da Garden of Eden? Ya?"

"Yes, sir."

"A wife is forever, Michael. And once you become a papa, you have a duty to da child and da woman who made dat child with you," his father told him. "Do you want to wake up each morning with dis girl by your side? Do you want dis girl like dat; forever?"

"No, I don't. But I wasn't thinking of that, Papa," Mike confessed.

"Exactly; dat is da problem. You weren't thinking. Isn't it time you use your brain first and think of things like dat before you start dis business in da hayloft?"

"Yes, sir. It is time I did."

"What will you do if she gets in da family way and says you are da father?"

"I don't know, Papa."

"Den, no time in da barn with any girl, eh?"

"Yes, sir. No more of that."

"Can I trust your word on dat, Michael?"

"Yes, sir. You can trust my word."

"I hope so, Michael. I hope so."

Jake turned to his younger son. "You listen to dis, son. Dis goes for you, too. You understand me?"

"Don't worry, Papa," Little Jake retorted. "Girls are yucky."

Jake laughed. "I'm happy to hear dat you still think so, son."

***

In the house, the girls were helping their mother clean up. Rose asked her daughter Ann about Louise Mohr.

"Ann," she began, "what did you hear about Michael and the Mohr girl?"

"I don't trust much of anything that girl says, Momma," Ann began. "She's always bragging about being in her barn with boys. Probably nothing happened with Michael."

"But, tell me what she said about Michael."

"She said that the two of them spent time alone in her barn."

"What's this alone in her barn business?"

"Oh, Momma," Ann blushed. "You know how we would never be alone with boys. Like that."

"Does that girl brag about being alone with other boys, too?"

Susan piped up. "She talks about that all the time, Momma. According to her, she has taken most of the older boys to her barn, except Carl Bacon. All the girls think he's creepy, even Louise."

"You do know that being intimate is how a girl can get in a family way, don't you?" Rose asked her daughters.

"Oh, Momma," Ann said, sort of chortling. "Of course we do."

"Don't worry about us, Momma," Susan assured her. "It's Michael you need to get after. Louise Mohr has her eye on him. She would love to get her hooks into him. She invited him to the barn with her twice, and he went."

"Would she get with child just to get Michael as a husband?" Rose asked.

"I wouldn't put it past her, Momma," Ann told her. "All the girls think Michael is the best catch around. So, whoever gets Louise in a family way wouldn't matter. I think she'd say Michael was the father. Don't you agree, Susan?"

"Ann's right, Momma," Susan answered. "Michael had best be careful, or we'll have a pregnant Louise to help us around this house."

Lowell School

"Good morning, everyone," Mr. Clingman began.

"Good morning, Mr. Clingman," all the students responded.

"Welcome to you all on this Monday morning. We are going to do things a bit differently today. On the blackboard, I have two lists of names. Ann Drieborg, you and your brother Jacob will work with the children on list number one in arithmetic. Mary Turbush, you and Thomas Rodammer will work with the children on list number two in reading. After an hour has passed, you will switch groups."

Mr. Clingman was a very active teacher. Five-foot-seven and slender, he seldom sat behind his desk. In fact, he was always moving around the room when he lectured. Even while the students worked at their desks, he was looking over their shoulders and could be found at the side of any student upon whose face he noticed a frown.

The children told their parents that he seemed to talk continuously. But they loved to listen to his stories. And he had stories for every occasion. He surely kept their attention. No one fell asleep in his classroom.

"This morning, the older students will work with me on current events," he continued. "I have gotten some old copies of the *Grand Rapids Eagle* newspaper and the *Weekly Enquirer* for us to use in our discussions. Mr. Spefford, owner of our Lowell weekly paper, will join us, too. Our subject will be the upcoming national elections.

"Ann and Jacob, take your group to that side of the room. Mary, you and Thomas use the other side of the room. Now, the rest of you come to the front. I want you to take a look at the map of the United States I've placed over the blackboard."

"Who can identify all the Slave States?"

Hands went up. He pointed to Ethan Schock. "You give it a try, Ethan. Point to each state and say it aloud, too."

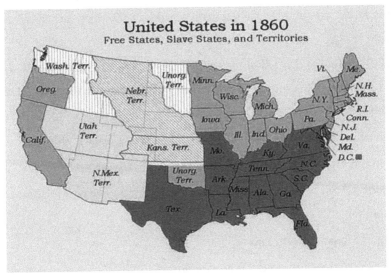

Ethan began and pointed to the map.

"South Carolina, Tennessee, Kentucky, North Carolina, Georgia, Mississippi, Louisiana, and Texas are all Slave States."

"Yes, sir. I think I know the ones he missed," Susan responded. But, before she answered, she looked at the map for a bit and began.

"Maryland, Florida, Missouri, Arkansas, Alabama, and Delaware are the Slave States, too."

"They are, Susan, but you've forgotten a very important one."

"Who knows the one she missed?"

"Virginia," a student shouted out.

"You have the correct answer, Carl, but you're supposed to raise your hand first. That's a rule of courtesy we all follow."

"Who cares about that silly rule? I knew the answer. That's all that counts."

"Mr. Bacon," Clingman corrected. "We live in an organized society where it is important for us to follow the rules and laws. Even little ones like raising your hand or taking turns. If you keep the little rules, the rest of us can be sure you will obey the big ones."

"My father says that the richest people make all the rules, and everybody else has to go along."

"We'll leave that discussion for another time, Carl. Right now, class, someone answer me this. What are the characteristics of the Slave States that make them different than the Free States?"

Several hands went up. "Mr. Drieborg," you take a crack at this one."

"I would say that the main difference is that slavery is legal in all those states."

"Correct," Mr. Clingman announced. "What kind of economy dominates the slave south?

"Mr. Turbush, do you know?"

"Yes sir," Ethan answered, "it is agriculture."

"Correct. In the North and West of this country, wheat and corn are the primary crops. What about the slave south?

"Susan, do you know?"

"I believe it is cotton, tobacco, rice, and sugar."

"That's correct, Susan. What do they do with all those crops?"

Mike's hand went up first.

"All right, Mr. Drieborg. You tell us."

"I think most of what they grow and harvest is exported either to the factories of our Northeast or England and Europe."

"Correct. And, let me impress upon you the importance of those exports to the wealth of the United States. Listen to this, students. For every dollar foreigners pay for goods we export, fifty cents goes to the Cotton South.

"That allows the people in the South to buy all sorts of goods and services. They buy grain from our West, giving our farmers a cash market. They also buy manufactured goods from the Northeast, providing employment to many thousands of workers there. Southerners also pay to have their goods shipped. This means that many people in New England have jobs as shipbuilders, and many others there are employed as sailors.

"Southerners also pay for insurance from companies in New York and Philadelphia, as well as paying interest on money borrowed from banks in the North. And, because the South purchases many of their manufactured goods from Europe, they pay our government a lot of taxes in tariffs."

Ethan raised his hand. "Yes, Mr. Schock, what is it?" his teacher asked.

"It sounds like you're saying that the economy of the United States needs the Cotton South to be prosperous."

"That's a great observation, Ethan," Mr. Clingman said, clapping his hands in approval. "You are exactly right. And don't forget, everyone, the people of the South need our grains and manufactured goods. So, we need each other.

"According to the last census, there were over eight million people in the Slave States and almost twenty million people in the Free States. Of those eight million in the South, guess how many of them are slaves?"

Carl Bacon interrupted, "Who cares about all of that?"

"Your father does, Mr. Bacon; here's why. His bank loans money to farmers and businessmen around this area. Grain grown in this area finds its way to the South to help feed the millions of people who live there. If they don't have the money to pay for the grain, they buy less, and the price per bushel will go down. Then, our farmers' incomes would decrease, they would spend less money in town, and our businessmen in Lowell would suffer. Then your father's loans could very well go unpaid. That's why your father cares about all this stuff, Carl."

Mr. Clingman continued to explain.

"The economy of the Northeast would suffer, too. If the cotton farmers have a bad crop, their exports decline, and so does their income. That will mean they will buy fewer of the goods manufactured in the factories of our Northeast. Unemployment will result, and that entire section will suffer. With less cotton, tobacco, rice, and sugar to ship, the sailors and ships of New England will not be as necessary. Unemployment will result there, too.

"So, you can see that the economy of the entire United States is dependent upon every section doing its part, just as Mr. Schock pointed out to us a few moments ago.

"Now, I want to focus on another facet of the problem.

"Who wants to hazard a guess about the number of slaves working in the South?

"Miss Hertzog? You've been silent all morning. What do you think? Of the eight million humans we believe live in the South, would you say one million are slaves?"

"A million is a lot, Mr. Clingman. I find it hard to imagine that many of anything, much less people. So, I'll just guess at a number. Since I think there would have to be more free people than slaves, I'll use your figure of one million slaves and seven million free people living in the Slave States."

"That is very good reasoning, Miss Hertzog," her teacher complimented. "But, in fact, the US Census of 1850 had almost three million of the eight million totals listed as slaves. Can you imagine that?

"What do they need all those millions of workers for, Miss Dittman?"

"I would suppose that number of slaves is needed to work in the fields."

"That's right, Sarah. The landowners can't get enough free white people to do that kind of work. It's been done by Negroes for over two hundred years. So now, it is considered beneath the dignity of free whites.

"Now tell me, class. What do the landowners of the South need to produce all this cotton, tobacco, rice, and sugar?"

"Miss Mohr? Do you know?"

"I haven't any idea, Mr. Clingman," she answered.

Carl Bacon interrupted again. "She's dumb as a stump. The only thing she knows anything about is taking boys to the barn."

The girls hid their smiles with their hands, and the boys laughed.

"I'll have none of that in this school," Mr. Clingman directed firmly.

"Mr. Bacon," he admonished. "I have told you before that you have no right to make fun of another student. I intend to write a note to your father about the unkind comment you made this day."

"My father won't care about any dumb note or about your silly rules, either. Remember, he's the head of the school board. He's your boss."

"Boss or not, you will follow the rules of this school as long as you're here, or you'll not be welcome."

"You can't kick me out, Clingman, 'cause I'm leaving right now. We'll see what my father has to say about this. Maybe you'll be the one kicked out."

Mr. Clingman addressed the rest of the students. "Stay in your seats, everyone. We'll resume our discussion after Mr. Bacon leaves."

After Carl Bacon left the building, Mr. Clingman turned his attention to his class and the last question he had asked. "What do the landowners in the South need to produce all that cotton, rice, tobacco, and sugar?"

Mike raised his hand. "Yes, Mr. Drieborg?"

"They need the same things we need, land, workers, and good weather."

"Correct, Michael. And who has been doing this kind of work in the South for the last two hundred years plus? Miss Dittman? Do you know?"

"The slaves have done it, Mr. Clingman," she answered.

"That's right, Sarah. So, class, it would seem that the South is very dependent upon slave labor to produce its farm products. Could that be why they are so upset over the possibility that their slaves could be freed by the act of Congress?

"Think about that for a few minutes while I check on the other children. Then, ponder this question: 'Should Congress act to end slavery in the entire United States?' We'll resume our conversation in fifteen minutes or so. Go ahead. Discuss this among yourselves."

The Harvey Bacon Home

Carl Bacon walked into his parents' Lowell home. His father was just leaving to go to his bank.

"You're supposed to be in school. What the devil are you doing home?" Harvey Bacon asked.

"Clingman threatened to write a note to you 'cause I said something he didn't like about a girl in our class. He told me I could leave if I didn't stop saying that kind of stuff. So I left. He's an ass, Daddy, and boring as the day is long. I can hardly stay awake in that place."

Mrs. Paula Bacon was standing at the end of the entryway, listening.

"What did you say, Carl?" she asked.

"You know that Mohr girl, Momma? I said that all she knew about was 'doing it' with boys in her papa's barn. Clingman got all steamed up and said I shouldn't say that kind of thing in his school. I only told the truth, Daddy."

"Clingman has overstepped his bounds this time, Paula," Harvey stormed. "He has no right to tell our boy to leave. Besides, it's not his school; he's only an employee."

Mrs. Bacon wasn't finished. "Did he tell you to leave, Carl?"

"He said I should leave his school if I continued to say things like that."

Mrs. Bacon turned to her husband. "Harvey," she began, "no student should be allowed to ridicule another student. I want you and me to take Carl back to that school right now for him to apologize to Mr. Clingman and the girl he insulted."

"Not me, Momma," Carl whined, "you can't make me do that."

"Harvey," she said sternly, "we should do this now."

"Truth is, Paula," Harvey said, "I'm already late for an important meeting at the bank. Our boy was only funning like school kids do. It's clear to me that

Clingman made a big deal of this to embarrass our son because I'm the school board president.

"If you think an apology from Carl is so damned important, you make him do it. I wash my hands of the entire mess." With that, he turned and walked out the front door.

Carl ran out the back door.

Lowell School

The schoolchildren were at their desks eating their lunches when Mrs. Bacon arrived. She walked up to Mr. Clingman, who was at his desk finishing his lunch.

"Excuse me for interrupting your lunch, Mr. Clingman," she began. "I wonder if I could talk to you in private."

"Of course, Mrs. Bacon. We can step outside if you wish."

"That would be fine."

Once out of earshot of the students, he turned to her. "How can I help you, ma'am?"

"First, I want to apologize for Carl's behavior this morning. I fully endorse the rules of conduct you demand of all the students here. They must learn to treat others with respect. You have my full support. I would have had Carl here to apologize, except he ran off. His father would be here, too, but he is tied up at the bank. In the future, if you have any complaints about Carl's behavior, please contact me."

"Yes, ma'am," Clingman responded. "I will be sure to keep you informed. Would you like to hear my opinion of what drives Carl to do these things?"

"Yes. I would, Mr. Clingman."

"Carl believes he is entitled to the respect and admiration of the other students because of his father's position as owner of the Lowell Bank and school board president. He does not realize that he must earn those things from his fellow students.

"So, he is always angry with them when they ignore him and treat him with contempt. Then he attempts to punish them with sarcasm. He rails against boys like Drieborg, Petzold, and Schock because they protect the girls and smaller students from his bully tactics. I believe he verbally attacked the Mohr girl because she refused to invite him to the barn, as she has so many other boys of Carl's age.

"One day, a student came to me and told me that Carl had killed a small dog out on the playground. Sure enough, he had thrown a large stone and killed a puppy. What appalled and angered the other students was that Carl was bragging about it and thought they should admire him for what he had done. After this incident, the girls called him 'Icky' Bacon.

"I believe he feels shunned by the other students, Mrs. Bacon. And worse, I think he knows that there is nothing he can do to change their perception of him. Children can be very cruel, you know.

"When I criticized Carl for his remarks about Miss Mohr today, I was also protecting him from the remarks I hear the other students make about him. All students must understand that such behavior is not acceptable in this school."

"Thank you for sharing with me, Mr. Clingman. I see these things as well. Unfortunately, Carl is eighteen. I doubt there is much I can do at this point to change his behavior. Hopefully, he will graduate soon. Then he will have a fresh start if he goes to the university."

"I hope so, ma'am. I must get back to my students now. Carl isn't the only high-energy boy in my school. Is there anything else?"

Mrs. Bacon smiled at that. "No, Mr. Clingman," she told him. "I have said what I came to say."

"Thank you for coming today and for your support, Mrs. Bacon."

The Drieborg Home

The Drieborg children were home from school. Susan and Ann were in the house.

"Anything interesting happen at school today, girls?" Rose asked her daughters.

The three of them were setting the table for supper. Their father and brother, Michael, would soon be done with the afternoon milking. Then they would wash up and be ready to eat. Jacob was out in the barn, too, doing what twelve-year-olds do and staying away from being told to do something or other by his older sisters.

Susan spoke first. "Right in the middle of Mr. Clingman's history lecture, Carl Bacon said that Louise Mohr was dumb and a tramp. Then he sassed our teacher and stormed out of school."

Rose just shook her head. "That poor child is very troubled. I feel sorry for his mother."

"She came to school this afternoon and talked with Mr. Clingman," Ann related. "They went outside to talk."

"Carl will be old enough to graduate soon. I know all the girls will be happy to see him go. He is so creepy. A month or so ago, Ann chased a ball during recess behind the schoolhouse. Carl was back there doing heaven knows what, and he grabbed Ann and tried to steal a kiss from her."

"I didn't know about that. What did you do, Ann?" her mother asked, a bit surprised.

"I slapped the creep across the face and gave him a good push. He tripped backward and whined that I had no call to hit him."

Susan added, "When Michael found out, he dragged Carl behind the schoolhouse after school and pounded on him real good. None of the girls have been bothered since."

Jake and his sons came into the house and took their seats at the table.

"Anybody would think a herd of cattle just came into the house, all the noise you three made," Ann kidded.

Rising to his sister's taunt, Little Jake responded, "That's what men do, smarty."

"You gotta ignore remarks like that, little brother," Mike urged him. "Ann only does it to aggravate you," he chuckled.

"Go ahead, Michael," Ann complained, "take all the fun out of my day."

Their mother stopped all the conversation. "That will be quite enough, children. We eat now. Say the grace, please, Susan. It is your turn."

"Yes, Momma."

The evening meal was the lightest meal of the day. Usually, leftovers from the noon dinner were served. Even so, dessert was always part of the meal. Tonight, it was pie, baked that day with newly picked apples.

With his coffee poured, Jake lit his pipe. "What lesson did Mr. Clingman teach today, Michael?" he asked.

"He spent the entire morning explaining the economic interdependence of the various sections of the United States and the dependence on slave labor in the Cotton South, Papa."

"Tell us about that, Susan," Rose asked. For the next half-hour or so, she and Michael repeated what they had learned that day.

"Thank you, children," Rose said. "It's as though we were in that classroom, isn't it, Papa?"

"But you didn't tell us what your discussion group decided about da need for slave labor in da Cotton South," Jake wondered.

Michael answered that one. "We told Mr. Clingman that because the production and sale of cotton, rice, and sugar were so important to the economic well-being of the country, the slave owners should be allowed to keep their slaves."

"So, your group would not abolish slavery?" Ann asked. "That is so terrible, Michael. I can't believe your group came up with that. How could you support slavery?"

Susan joined the discussion. "There is no alternate supply of labor in the South, Ann. Without slaves, there would be little cotton, rice, or sugar produced. Certainly not enough to support the economies of the West and Northeast, anyway. So, we said we supported Mr. Lincoln's position to leave slavery alone where it is but prevent its spread elsewhere."

"Well said, Susan," her father said. "You two are learning a lot about how our country works, aren't dey, Momma?"

"Yes, I am very proud of them, Papa," Rose commented.

"Michael, would you get the book *Uncle Tom's Cabin* from the shelf for me?"

When Michael returned to the table with the book, his father said, "I want to hear that part about the chasing of runaway slaves again. Can you find that part, son?"

Michael leafed through the pages. "I think I have it, Papa," he announced.

"Don't read it all. Just tell us about it some."

"Well," Michael began, "it seems that state Senator John Bird arrived home one evening. His wife began to chide him for voting for a bill that required citizens to stop aiding runaway slaves and even requiring them to put runaways in jail to await their return to their former condition. When he said it was unfortunate but his duty to do so, she said to him,

"Duty, John! Don't use that word! You know it isn't a duty — it can't be a duty!"

"Dat's enough, son," Jake said. "You can stop reading. Dey are talking about 'Da Fugitive Slave Act' our congress passed. It says it is our duty to capture and turn in runaway slaves, just like you read in da book. I saw some of dat kind of treatment back in Holland with runaway peasants. I don't think I could obey dat law. Would you want me to, Momma?"

"No, Papa. I wouldn't."

The children just listened as their father continued. "When Ann and I were in town da odder day, one of da men at the elevator said he read in his Bible dat it is God's will dat da Negro is a slave and must serve da white man. This man said dat we must resign ourselves to slavery and support its existence everywhere.

"Dis point of view troubles me very much. I can't believe dis is da will of God. We should ask our pastor what he thinks of dis point of view, eh?"

Jake stopped talking and began packing fresh tobacco in his pipe.

Rose stood up from the table and announced, "Enough of this discussion for now, everyone. We have the dishes to take care of, girls. Boys, we need some firewood for the morning baking."

"And boys," Jake added, "don't forget to empty da chamber pots before it gets dark."

"I so hate that," Little Jake grumbled to himself, *"why can't my sisters empty those smelly pots for once?"*

The Bacon Home

At their supper table, the Bacons were having a much different conversation.

"I don't care what you say, Mother. I will not return to that school. Clingman lets everyone pick on me, and I don't learn anything anyways."

His thirteen-year-old sister Theresa piped in, "I think Mr. Clingman is the best teacher we have ever had in our school, Papa. I learn a lot from him. I get along with everyone and enjoy school a lot, too. Carl is just mad that the other boys don't let him run things and that he's upset that all the girls think he's weird."

"Listen to me, son," his mother continued. "If you intend to go to the University of Michigan, you must graduate from the Lowell school first," she reminded him.

At this point, Harvey Bacon entered the conversation.

"I'm the president of the Lowell School Board, Paula. I'll just make out a certificate of graduation for Carl. He can get into the university this December. He won't even have to return to our hick school."

"But Papa," Theresa revealed, "Carl doesn't do his lessons in school or turn in homework now. How will he ever be able to do his studies at the university?"

"Tattletale!" Carl shouted at his sister.

"First things first," Harvey Bacon said. "First, we get him into the university, then we get him a place to stay. We'll worry about classes and homework later."

"Harvey," Paula Bacon objected, "I don't think it's a good idea to arrange this for Carl. Our daughter is right. He hasn't even demonstrated he is willing to do schoolwork in what you call a hick school. Will he be able to do the work required at the University of Michigan?"

"He's my son, for God's sake. He'll be just fine."

Lowell Bank

Jake Drieborg was sitting in a straight-backed chair in the entryway of the Lowell Bank. He had an eight o'clock appointment with the owner, Harvey Bacon.

Five-foot-four Harvey would have to tip his head back to look Jake in the eye. So, when Jake was ushered into the bank president's office, the chair he was directed to use was virtually six inches off the floor. And Bacon's desk sat on an elevated platform so he could look down on those who sought a loan.

He did not rise as Jake entered his office or extend his hand with a welcoming handshake.

"Sit down, Drieborg. The file I have here tells me everything I need to know about you," Bacon began. There was no greeting like 'good morning' or 'how can I help you' from Bacon.

Jake could feel the heat of anger on the back of his neck.

This is a cruel man, this Bacon. He has control of the money I need, and he wants me to know it. He wants me to beg before he loans me the money I need to buy equipment. If I could have gone anyplace else for the money, I would have. But everybody knows no other bank will even accept a Lowell person's request for a loan; we have to deal with Bacon. He knows it, too."

"You know, of course, that no other bank around here would loan you a penny without my say-so. You know that, don't you, Drieborg?"

"Yes, I do."

"What did you just say? I didn't quite hear you."

This is worse than the last time I was here. He wants me to beg," Jacob thought.

"I know I must borrow any funds I need from you, Mr. Bacon."

"That's better. I just wanted to make sure you knew why you were here."

"So, you want to borrow another $300 to buy a steel plow, a drill, and a threshing machine? Is that it?"

"Yes, sir."

"I'm to add this amount to the mortgage you have with this bank, I take it. Is that right?"

"Yes, sir."

"Why?"

"Why, sir?" Jake responded, puzzled by the question.

"Don't play games with me, Drieborg," Bacon almost shouted. "Why do you think you need to buy this farm equipment?"

"Dese three pieces of equipment will allow me to plow more quickly dan I do now. With dem, I can plant more acres in da time it takes me to plant fewer, like now. If I plant more acres, I'll have to harvest more acres, too. So, da thresher will be needed at dat time."

"Where are you gonna sell this increased crop? Seems to me you'll just create a surplus, so you won't get any more for your crop at all, maybe even less. What've you got to say to that?"

"My additional bushels of wheat and corn will not affect da overall market, Mr. Bacon. It will be only a thimble-full overall. But, with da political crises that I believe are coming in dis country, I think da demand for grains will go up, not down. So, da price per bushel should rise, too."

"So, you're an economic genius now, are you?"

"No, sir," Jake replied. Then he repeated his prediction. "I believe der will be increased demand for grains in da near future. Prices will go up. So some money can be made by dose people who are prepared. With my increased acreage under cultivation next spring, I will be one of dose who is ready to take advantage of da situation in my small way."

"But tell me, Drieborg," Bacon leaned forward, arms on his desk, "what are you gonna do about that bully son of yours?"

"What is he talking about? Is dis about a schoolyard fight our boys had, maybe?"

"I don't know what you are talking about, Mr. Bacon."

Bacon stood behind his desk. Now, Jake had to look up to him. That's the way Bacon liked it.

"Not long ago, my son came home with a bloody nose and looking a mess. It appears that your son gave him a beating at school. You mean to tell me you don't know what goes on in your own family?"

"I didn't know about our sons getting into a fight, no."

"How can I trust you with this bank's money if you can't be trusted to properly supervise your children? Or to discipline them when they step out of line? Eh?

"Tell you what, Drieborg," Bacon continued, "in the past, you've paid your debts on time. I like your reasoning on this equipment proposal, too. So, I'm inclined to give you the loan at the usual rates, of course. But we need to clear up this business of your out-of-control son.

"We are going to have a school assembly soon. There, in front of everybody, your son is going to apologize to my son Carl for the beating he gave him. Do we have an understanding, Drieborg?"

Jake thought about this.

"The Bacon boy is nothing but trouble. Michael has been told repeatedly to stay away from him. I have to agree to this condition if I am to get the loan I need. But, as hard as it is for me to make Michael do this, it might not be a bad thing, after all; the embarrassment of having to apologize like this may teach Michael that there are consequences to his actions. It may do my son some good," Jacob decided.

"Yes, sir," Jake agreed, "Michael will apologize to your son at dis school assembly."

Bacon smiled broadly. "I thought you might see it my way, Drieborg."

The Harvest Dance

"Momma!" Susan complained. "Why do I have to have my dance dress the same color and material as Ann's?"

"Your dress will be just as beautiful as your sister's, Susan," Rose told her daughter, "just you wait and see. Do you think I would not have you looking your best? My goodness."

Rose was using the same color and material for both dresses. But she had gotten a different pattern for each dress. And while white lace decorated the sky blue of Susan's dress, a different lace pattern was used on Ann's.

"They will soon see," she thought. *"Everyone will admire their dresses. They will see. My boys are ever so much less trouble. They would wear their barn clothing if I let them."*

***

The Fall Harvest dance was held at the Lowell schoolhouse. The children's desks were piled at one side of the large room. Fiddlers stood on the raised platform where Mr. Clingman's desk usually sat.

Mothers sat in straight-backed chairs along the opposite wall, and most of the men were outside smoking and talking about crops and the upcoming election for president. They were also standing outside the door to make sure none of their children snuck away from the dance for some alcohol or a romantic meeting.

The young boys Jacob's age were chasing around, not at all interested in the dancing. The young girls his age danced with one another. Mike and the older boys were standing in a group by the piled-up desks, hands in their pockets. None of them wanted to be the first to ask a girl to dance.

The girls their age weren't much better; clustered on the other side of the room, they pretended not to notice the boys.

That didn't last long, though. After several dance numbers had been played, Susan and Ann Drieborg walked across the room toward the boys.

Susan took Willie Petzold by the arm and virtually dragged him onto the dance floor. Once he got there and she took him into her arms, he evidently found it a pleasant experience because he stopped struggling.

Ann did the same with Ethan Schock. He balked a bit, but she wouldn't let go. So, he gave in and joined her in the middle of the floor.

As she had pulled him out of the group of boys, Mike said:

"I see that ring in your nose, Schock. She's got you now."

Not to be outdone, Sarah Dittman was right behind the Drieborg girls. She grabbed onto Mike like a tiger with prey in its jaws.

"Come on, Drieborg, you and I are going to dance," she told him.

Schock laughed when Mike and Sarah danced by. "Who's got a ring in his nose now, Drieborg?"

Fall Hunting

School was out for the weekend. Michael and two of his friends were tramping through the woods, hunting deer. Each boy held a muzzleloader across his chest, ready to aim and fire quickly. The snow on the ground had come early this year.

"This new snow won't last very long today, but right now, it makes it easy to spot deer tracks," Willie Turbush told his two friends.

Ethan Schock snapped, "Your loud voice makes it easier for the deer to hear us coming, too."

"Hey, Ethan," Mike asked, "you danced with my sister Ann at the Harvest Dance. Are you serious about her?"

"Naw, not really," he responded. "She's pretty and all. But she's too bossy for me. You know what I mean?"

Mike chuckled, "Sure do, Ethan. I sure do."

"What about you and Dittman?" Willie asked. "You sure danced a lot with her that night. You take her to the barn, Mike?"

"Come on, Petzold," Mike said. "she's not like that. She's a nice girl. Besides, I promised my papa not to do that. I'm going to wait until I'm married to the girl."

"What's not to like about Sarah?" Ethan asked. "She's pretty and smart, too."

"I've decided I'm not ready to start a family yet. Maybe I will be ready in a year or two, though," Mike responded.

"I thought we were hunting today. Or are we going to talk about girls instead?" Willie asked his friends.

"Don't get your shorts in an uproar, Petzold," Mike kidded. "You're just irritated you only got to dance with my sister Susan a few times; the older guys sort of cut you out."

"If you're finished, Drieborg," Petzold snapped, "can we get on with our hunting?"

"All right, take it easy. Let's spread out," Mike agreed.

"Right," Ethan agreed. "I'll go to our right about twenty yards. What will you two do?"

"How about you stay on this path, Willie? I'll go to your left about twenty yards," Mike suggested.

"That's fine with me," Willie responded. "Just remember, you two, I'm in the middle, so don't shoot in my direction."

"Wouldn't think of it, Willie," Michael promised. "We need you to take my place beating up on that creep Bacon. I promised my parents I wouldn't do it anymore."

All the boys laughed. "That's right," Ethan said. "I thought I'd die when you had to apologize in front of everyone at the school Christmas assembly. Why did you do that, Mike?"

"My father asked old man Bacon for a loan a few weeks ago. As a condition, Bacon insisted that I apologize. I told you all this; don't you remember?"

"Ya, I guess so," Willie admitted. "Sure was funny, though. I didn't know whether to laugh or cry listening to you up on that stage fumbling with the words."

"For crying out loud, Willie. Thanks a lot. I knew I could count on you to understand. I only did it so my father could get his loan. I didn't do it because I meant it."

"I thought you did a beautiful job, Mikie," Ethan teased. "I was really impressed by your sincere apology."

Mike threw a snowball at his friend. That started a storm of snowballs between the three boys.

Exhausted, the three lay in the snow, breathing hard.

"The next time Bacon picks on one of the girls or the little people, it will be your turn to pound on him back of the schoolhouse, Ethan," Mike reminded him. "Then we'll see who has to apologize next time."

"You've forgotten, Drieborg," Willie said, "our friend Carl was given a graduation diploma. So, we'll not see him at the Lowell school anymore."

"Ya," Ethan said, "when I was working at Zania's general store last Saturday, I heard he's headed for the University of Michigan after Christmas.

"He saw me on my way home from school the other day. He said he was gonna get even some day for all the beatings I gave him. But once he's at the university, he'll be their problem."

"Good riddance," Willie concluded.

The boys got up and resumed their hunt. It wasn't long before Mike saw a deer feeding on a sapling twenty or thirty yards ahead. His shot was accurate, and the deer dropped after it had run only a few feet.

Mike shouted at Willie, and he, in turn, yelled to Ethan. The boys gathered around the dead animal.

"Can't say you got a very big one, Mike," Willie judged. "See those tiny horns. It was hardly worth shooting."

"Oh, is that right?" Mike responded. "And where is your deer, Willie, my friend? If we don't get another before dark, are you going to refuse your share of this one?"

"Gosh, you get mad quick, Drieborg. Keep a lid on it, will you?"

"Just asking, Willie," Mike teased," Come on, you two. We've got a couple of hours of light left."

"Maybe we can get another deer before we have to quit," Ethan added.

They did not spot another deer before dark. Mike's shot had probably frightened the rest of the deer into hiding. So they gutted the animal Mike shot where it lay. Mike cut a sapling, tied the deer's legs to it, and his two friends carried the carcass out of the woods.

It wasn't far to the Drieborg barn, where they intended to hang the carcass from a beam to drain.

"Hi, Mr. Drieborg," Willie said as he and Ethan carried the deer carcass into the Drieborg barn.

Mike's father was finishing the afternoon milking. Little Jake was in the stall next to him. It was his turn to help his father.

Jake saw the carcass as the boys walked by and commented. "Pretty small animal, don't you think, boys?"

Willie howled, and Ethan joined in the laughter.

Mike's face reddened. "Can we hang it on that beam in the empty stall, Papa?"

"Sure, boys. Don't leave it more than two days, though. Let it drain for now. But you need to skin and butcher it soon. All right, son?"

"Yes, Papa," Mike promised.

"After you hang da deer, Michael, clean yourself real good before you come in da house," he directed. "Mamma's got supper ready, so don't be long. You know how she gets when anyone is late."

"Yes, Papa," Mike responded.

His two friends were in the back stall, hanging the deer carcass. They could hardly complete the job; they were laughing so hard about the small deer remark Mike's father had made. Finally, Mike arrived and wrestled them to the ground.

"You think that's funny, eh?" he said as he held Willie down, grabbed Ethan by a leg, and pulled him onto the pile.

"Let us up, Mike," Willie shouted. "Your momma's going to be mad if you're late for supper."

"That's the only reason I'm letting you off easy, Turbush," Mike said in mock anger.

"What about Schock?" Willie complained. "He's laughing as hard as me."

"You just wait. I'll find a way to get even with both of ya. Believe me, I will," Mike promised. " Now get out of here. I've still got to clean up."

It wasn't long before Mike took his seat at the supper table.

His little brother Jacob made a remark.

"The great hunter has returned, everyone."

Susan asked, "What is that supposed to mean?"

Little Jake told her, "Michael killed a deer today that was not much bigger than our dog. It was hardly worth dragging it back to the barn if you ask me," he chuckled.

"No one asked you, squirt," Mike snapped.

"No more of that at my table, children," Rose cautioned.

"Maybe, Jacob, you don't want any of those deer steaks when I cook them, eh? I think you should apologize to your brother, don't you?"

"Aw, Momma," he said. "I'm sorry, Mike."

Ann whispered to her big brother, "Was it really tiny, Michael?"

"Shut up about it, will you?"

Ann and Susan chuckled, too.

October Election Parade

The morning milking and chores had been done, but Jake had not gone to Lowell as he usually did on Saturday morning. Instead, everyone had been directed to clean up and dress in their Sunday best for a special trip to Grand Rapids.

"Come on, everybody," Rose Drieborg shouted to no one in particular, "It's time to go."

"Do I have to wear these clothes?" Jacob complained. "Can't I just wear my ordinary stuff?"

Susan looked at her young brother. "Jacob," she said in exasperation, "we're going to hear Mr. Lincoln give a speech. You need to look your best."

"What the heck do I care about some speech? I bet your Mr. Lincoln doesn't care how I dress, anyway. I'd rather stay home and play with my friends any day."

"Maybe so, Jacob, but you're not staying home today. You heard Momma. So lace up your shoes 'cause we're leaving right now."

"Bossy!" Jacob responded.

"Want me to tell Papa you're not ready?"

"Oh, all right."

It had been some time since Jake and Rose had been to Grand Rapids. Last year they had traveled in that direction with their children on their way to the village of Sparta.

They had planned to visit Rose's sister, Margaret, who lived there. Sparta was a small farm town just north of Grand Rapids. It was much like their village of Lowell. They stayed overnight that time. That was a real treat. The Drieborg children had had a great time getting acquainted with their eight cousins.

Today though, they traveled on Fulton Street and headed into Grand Rapids, the second-largest city in Michigan. Located on both sides of the Grand River, it was a major center for the lumber industry. It was estimated that almost 10,000 people resided there in 1860.

Following a parade, Abraham Lincoln would give a campaign speech there this afternoon. Grand Rapids would be the first speech on his trip. He would give another speech in Lansing, Michigan's capital, and finally one in Detroit.

"Are you going to vote Republican this time, Papa?" Michael asked.

"I voted Democrat last time, son," he answered. "Four years ago, I thought Mr. Buchanan was da best man. So, I voted Democrat.

"But, dis time, I'm thinking dis new Republican party might be a better one to lead our country. So, last week I voted for da Republican candidate for Congress, Mr. Kellogg. I might just vote for dis Abraham Lincoln, da Republican candidate for president. We'll see. Dat's why we're here. I want to hear da man speak for himself, not just read about what he believes in da newspaper."

Ann spoke up, "Why are you going, Momma? You can't vote."

"Maybe I can't cast my own vote, daughter," Rose responded somewhat testily, "but before your papa votes, we will talk about who we think is the best man for the country. So, when Papa casts his vote, it will be for the two of us. That's why I want to hear Mr. Lincoln for myself. Do you understand, Ann?"

"It would be better if you could cast your own vote, seems to me."

"But I can't. So your papa and I make the best of it."

"I suppose."

Signs directed Jake to park his wagon just off Fountain Street. Then the family walked down the hill toward the river. The speaker's stand was located on the bank of the river. Rose looked for a good spot from which to hear the speeches.

Suddenly, she stopped and put her blanket on the ground. "This should be a good spot, Papa."

"Put the food baskets on the edge of the blanket, girls," Rose directed. "Papa, check the newspaper for the time of the parade."

"Da paper says it starts at 11 o'clock at da top of da Fulton Street hill and will come down to da river at da front of the speaker's platform on Monroe Street. " Jake took out his pocket watch. "It is now 10:30, Momma."

"Thank you, Papa," she responded. "Leave the food here. Come, children, we had better hurry over if we're going to get a good place to watch the parade. Come, Papa."

The family had arrived none too soon. Thousands of people lined Fulton Street hill and all the way along Monroe Street to the river. The Drieborgs had to look over two rows of people standing on the wooden sidewalk. The other side of the street was filled with people, too.

At exactly 11 AM, a band could be heard, and then another. Over the crest of Fulton Street, half a mile away from where they stood, men appeared carrying a big banner that stretched clear across the street. Then came the first band, followed by a wagon filled with men. Another banner appeared, and another band and another wagonload of men.

"You have da good eyes, Momma," Jake said. "What's da banner say on it?"

"It says 'Free Men,' Papa."

The second banner came into view. "This one says, 'Free Labor,' Papa."

"And da next one?"

"The third one says 'Free Soil.'"

The third band and wagonload of men came over the crest of Fulton Street, and yet another banner came into view.

"This new one says 'Vote Lincoln,' Papa."

Little Jake was sitting on Michael's shoulders. "Hey!" he shouted. "Look at those men carrying rails on their shoulders."

"I can't see, Jacob," his brother said. "I read that those men are called 'Wide Awakes.' There are supposed to be tens of thousands of them all across the Northern states. How many do you see?"

Little Jake tried to count them. "I lose count. But there must be hundreds of them, Michael. And a lot of them are carrying a wooden rail. Is that why they call Lincoln the 'Rail Splitter' ?"

"Yes. I guess he split rails when he was a young guy. He worked with his hands, they say," Mike told his brother.

"Look at those girls walking alongside the bands, Ann," Susan said, pointing to the first band as it approached their spot. They were girls about her age, dressed in white with red and blue sashes. "What are they throwing to the people?"

"I don't know. I'll try to catch one." She did. "It's a piece of toffee, Susan."

Up and down the street, kids were scrambling for the candy. From his perch on Mike's shoulders, Little Jake caught one thrown high over the crowd.

"I got one, Mike! I got one!" he shouted.

"Good for you, little brother. Get one for me when the next band comes by."

"Listen to the chanting, Momma," Susan said.

The men in the wagons had bull horns that could be heard shouting:

"Free Men! Free Labor! Free Land!"

The people in the crowd along Fulton Street picked it up:

"Free Men: Free Labor: Free Land: Lincoln," they chanted. Again and again, they shouted the refrain, encouraged by the men in the wagons who used the bullhorns to direct the chant toward the crowd.

The Drieborg children joined the chant and clapped their hands in unison with the beat:

"Free Men! Free Labor! Free Land!"

It took a good hour for the parade to pass the Drieborgs. Then, as each band reached the riverside at the foot of Fulton Street, it moved behind the speaker's stand. The banners and wagons of cheerleaders followed and took their places alongside the stand to face the audience.

As the crowd moved to take places on the hill looking down at the speaker's stand, the cheerleaders left their wagons and faced the audience with their bullhorns.

Once again, they took up the chant

"Free Men! Free Labor! Free Land!"

The leaders divided the crowd into cheering sections and encouraged each section to out-shout the other with the chant.

The crowd on the left shouted, "Free Men."

The crowd in the center shouted, "Free Labor."

The crowd right shouted, "Free Land."

Then everyone shouted, "Vote Lincoln."

The shouting continued until the people simply grew tired of it and stopped. The children saw school friends and wandered away from their families.

"There's Ethan Schock," Ann said."

"And Willie Turbush is here with his family, too," Susan observed.

"Michael," she continued. "I see Sarah Dittman. Are you going to talk with her?"

"Why? I see her every day in school."

"This is different, Michael," Susan instructed her older brother. "Besides, it would be a polite thing for you to do."

"I don't see your precious Willie coming over to talk with you; or Ethan, looking for Ann, either."

"Michael Drieborg," she snapped, "I'll take care of my business; you take care of yours if you please."

Mothers all over the hill directed their families to sit and eat before the speeches started.

"Come, everyone," Rose directed. "We have cold chicken casserole, jam and bread to eat; fruit, too. Susan, you fill the cups with water. Ann, get the napkins for everyone, please. I'll serve the casserole. Don't forget we have rhubarb pie for dessert."

It had been several hours since their seven o'clock breakfast, so everyone was hungry. The boys wolfed down Rose's chicken casserole. Even their father, Jake, had a second helping. As much as they ate, they still had room for the pie. The girls enjoyed the picnic meal but were much more restrained.

As soon as Rose and the girls packed the plates, cups, silverware, and leftovers in the basket, Jake walked the baskets back to their wagon. When he returned, he stretched out on the family blanket and closed his eyes. The children wandered away in search of friends. It wasn't long, though, before the bands came alive down by the speaker's stand.

"Papa," Rose nudged him, "look, I see men going up the steps of the speaker's platform. The way they're dressed, I think they're important people. Wake up, Papa; it's almost time to start!"

The children rejoined their parents.

"Where did you get the American flags, children?" Rose asked.

"The men of the Wide Awakes are going through the crowd passing them out, Momma," Ann told her. "I think it's starting."

Sure enough, the cheerleaders ran to the front of the platform and began shouting into their megaphones:

"Lincoln! Lincoln! Lincoln!"

They pumped their arms up and down, urging everyone to stand. More and more of the crowd caught the message. At first, hundreds joined the chant, then thousands stood and joined the chant. The hill was awash with American flags being waved, too.

"Lincoln! Lincoln! Lincoln!"

After a few minutes, a horse-drawn coach pulled up and stopped in front of the platform. A tall man stepped out and waved his stovepipe hat to the crowd.

"Lincoln! Lincoln! Lincoln!"

The thousands standing on the hill went wild with cheering as Lincoln mounted the steps and faced the crowd with his hands raised. The chanting went on and on:

"Lincoln! Lincoln! Lincoln!"

"Papa," Rose shouted. "That's really Lincoln! How exciting, Papa!"

"Yes, Momma, it really is. We will hear him speak as soon as da crowd quiets down, I think."

It took some time, and the crowd did quiet some. Most of the people who had been standing wanted to hear Lincoln speak, too. So they stopped cheering.

A person stood on the stage holding a sign. It announced the first speaker.

Governor Austin Blair

"Look at that man coming to the railing on the speaker's platform," Susan said to no one in particular.

"The sign says he's our new governor."

Governor Blair addressed the crowd. "Ladies and gentlemen. Can I can have your attention, please?"

He paused, and the crowd quieted down some. Then the governor began to speak.

"First, allow me to thank you for electing me governor of our great state of Michigan. Second, I also thank you for electing a Republican state legislature. Together we will carry out our promises. And, together, we look forward to working with the new Republican Congress in Washington City, our new Congressman, William Kellogg, and our United States Senator, Zachariah Chandler."

Senator Chandler moved to the platform's railing and waved to modest applause.

The governor continued. "We are here in Grand Rapids today on the first stop of our journey across the state of Michigan. Yet this afternoon, we will speak to the people of the Lansing area. And tonight, we will have a torchlight parade in our state's largest city, Detroit.

"On election day this November 6th, it is my hope that you will also give us a Republican president."

The cheerleaders jumped up again and began to chant:

"Lincoln! Lincoln! Lincoln!"

Primed now, the crowd rose and joined them, clapping, shouting, and waving their American flags.

"Lincoln! Lincoln! Lincoln!"

The governor held up his hands again, asking for the crowd to be quiet. After the shouting subsided, he continued.

"Today, it is my privilege to share this stage with the next president of the United States, Abraham Lincoln!"

The Wide Awakes ran in front of the platform with the cheerleaders. Thousands in the crowd once again came to their feet. They needed no urging this time. In one voice, they shouted:

"Lincoln! Lincoln! Lincoln!

This time no amount of urging by the governor could quiet the crowd. They went on and on with the chant.

"Lincoln! Lincoln! Lincoln!"

Only when the Wide Awakes and the cheerleaders finally sat down did the crowd follow suit and sit.

"Thank you, everyone," Governor Blair continued. "Abraham Lincoln is the only candidate for president who rose from poverty by working the soil and working with his hands. He is the only candidate for president who has always opposed the extension of slavery to the territories. He is the only candidate for president who has pledged to protect the free workers of the North from the competition of slave labor. He is the only candidate for president who has publicly condemned the Fugitive Slave Act, the Dred Scott decision, and the Kansas-Nebraska Act. He is the only candidate for president who has pointed out the moral evil of slavery.

"Without further delay, it gives me great pleasure to introduce the Rail Splitter from Illinois, the champion of free men, free labor, and free soil, Abraham Lincoln!"

The governor turned and welcomed the much taller Lincoln to the front railing of the platform. He stepped back as Lincoln moved forward. When Lincoln raised his arms to the crowd, the thousands seated to his front rose to their feet in a thunderous roar that seemed to echo off the hill on which they stood. Everyone was clapping and shouting again and again:

"Lincoln! Lincoln! Lincoln!"

There was no stopping them now. They seemed consumed in a frenzy, cheering their Lincoln. If there was anyone in the crowd who was not for Lincoln, no one could tell. Everyone was swept up in the cheering, clapping, and chanting. The hill was again awash with American flags. Not even Lincoln could quiet them. So he gave up trying and gave himself to the crowd for a full five, ten, and then fifteen minutes. Only when they seemed exhausted did individuals at first and then groups of people begin to sit on the hillside. Only then was the crowd quiet.

Lincoln began to speak.

"Thank you, thank you, for the warm Michigan welcome. I have stepped out upon this platform that I may see you and that you may see me, and in the arrangement, I have the best of the bargain.

"I come here today as a man born and bred in the West. I'm a man born to the land. I'm one who had to work with his hands to survive. I know what it is like to rise before daylight and to work under a hot sun until evening. I know what it is like to go to bed hungry as well.

"And, after I left the land, there were times when I lost work because slaves were available to do the same job.

"If slavery is right, all words, acts, laws, and constitutions against it are themselves wrong and should be silenced and swept away.

"But, if it is wrong, it should not be allowed to spread. That is what this election is all about.

"I am here today to tell you that slavery is wrong. It is a violation of God's eternal plan, a detestable crime, and ruinous to this nation. Those who deny freedom to others deserve it not for themselves and, under the rule of a just God, cannot long retain it.

"And, I believe that the spreading out and perpetuity of the institution of slavery impairs the general welfare of our nation. I believe - nay, I know that that is the only thing that has ever threatened the perpetuity of the Union itself.

"For, if the safeguards of liberty are broken down now to allow slavery everywhere, how long before the rights of others, say poor white men, are put in question?

"Believe me when I pledge to you this day that the slavers will not prevail in this election. And, I pledge to you that as president, I will protect free men everywhere. There will be no slaves taking the jobs of working people in the Free States of this country. And, there will be no slaves in the territories of this country."

Thousands jumped to their feet again. This time, they needed no urging from the cheerleaders to voice their support for Lincoln. They knew the Rail Splitter was one of them, and as president, he would protect them from those who wanted to see slavery everywhere in the United States.

"Lincoln! Lincoln! Lincoln!"

Lincoln's final words to the crowd in Grand Rapids were:

"I leave you today hoping that the lamp of liberty will burn in your bosoms until there shall no longer be a doubt that all men are created free and equal as God intended."

After waving to the crowd, Lincoln was escorted from the platform and whisked away in his covered carriage to the cheering of the crowd.

"Lincoln! Lincoln! Lincoln!"

The Ride Home

The Drieborg wagon was finally free of the crowded streets of Grand Rapids. It had taken a good half-hour just to get through the crowd to their wagon. Then they had to get behind a long line of wagons struggling to get up the steep Fountain Street hill. Once out of that heavy traffic, Jake cut over to Fulton Street to head east toward Lowell.

"Wasn't Lincoln wonderful, Momma?" Ann said to her mother.

"Yes, I think so, Ann," her mother answered. "What do you think, Susan?" she asked her elder daughter.

"Oh, I agree with you. His speech left no doubt where he stood about the spread of slavery."

Mike interrupted. "It's no wonder the leaders of the South are afraid of his possible election. Mr. Clingman told us in school that Lincoln could be elected president even if the voters in the South didn't vote for him.

"Were you impressed by Lincoln, Papa?" Mike asked.

"Yes, I was, son. He told us about his working background. Dat he believes slavery is da biggest issue in dis election. Why he thinks slavery is wrong and what he will do about it if he is elected. He could not have been clearer. I liked dat."

"Well, Papa," Mike asked, "do you agree with him about slavery?"

"You know," Jake began, "before all dis election business started, I wasn't concerned about slavery too much. It seemed far away in da South, you know. And besides, we lived in a Free State. So why should I be worried about it?

"But den I listened to our priest when he told us that our freedoms come from God, not men. And, I began to wonder why some men like me have dese freedoms, but da Negroes do not. Aren't dey God's children, too?

"Den I thought, if men can take away freedom from dem, could men decide to take away dese freedoms from me too, maybe? So, when Mr. Lincoln says all men are created equal, I think he includes Negroes, too; and dat he will also protect me from having my freedoms taken away.

"When I read dat da Supreme Court in Washington decided dat because slaves are property der owners can take dem anywhere in our country, I realized dat if Lincoln loses dis election, we might not be protected from having slavery here in Michigan.

"We could have slavery right here, just like in Georgia or South Carolina, and I would have to help people keep der property. To keep people in chains, in slavery.

"I don't think I could do dat, children. I don't think I want to do dat. So, I think we should vote for dis Mr. Lincoln. What about you, Momma? Should we vote for dis Mr. Lincoln?"

"Yes, Papa," Rose said, "I think we should vote for this Mr. Lincoln."

"Hooray! Hooray!" Susan and Ann cheered and clapped from the wagon's second bench seat and leaned forward to hug their parents, too.

"Watch out, Susan," her papa said in pretended anger. "I have to keep our wagon on da road here." But he was smiling when he said it.

That night Susan sat in bed. Her sister was under the covers reading by the light on her side. Susan was telling her diary about the exciting day.

***

Dear Diary

What a wonderful day I had in Grand Rapids today. The whole family was there to hear Mr. Lincoln talk. There was a great big parade, all kinds of banners and flags, too. We had a picnic lunch on one of the hills surrounding the city, looking down on the speaker's stand by the river. It was so thrilling — everyone shouting and clapping. Mr. Lincoln was wonderful. Papa was so impressed he is going to vote for him. The election isn't very far away. I'll let you know how it turns out. Susan

The Election

In the very early hours of November 7, 1860, Abraham Lincoln arrived home from a long day at the telegraph office. Despite his weariness, he had a spring in his step as he climbed the steps to awaken his wife. Once inside their bedroom, he shook her awake gently.

"Mary, Mary," he whispered, "we've been elected president."

The next day it was announced across the nation that in March 1861, Abraham Lincoln would be sworn in as the 16th President of the United States.

***

In the Lowell schoolhouse, Mr. Clingman stood in front of his students, holding a copy of the previous day's *Grand Rapids Eagle* newspaper.

"According to the paper, there is no longer any doubt that Lincoln was elected president. Senator Douglas, the Democratic candidate, was second in the popular vote; Breckenridge, the Cotton South candidate, was third; and Bell, the Union candidate, was fourth.

"Lincoln did not receive a clear majority of the popular vote, but he did receive the 152 Electoral Votes required for election. The writer of this article says that the Democrat, Douglas, would have won if the other two men had not gotten so many votes in the South from people who would have normally voted for the Democratic candidate.

"Mr. Lincoln wasn't even on the ballot in most of the Slave States. So, it would appear that he was elected by voters in the Free States alone. It is no wonder, then, that the Southern press is calling him the 'Yankee President.'

Mr. Clingman continued. "Late in the evening of November 6th, Lincoln had won 145 Electoral votes. If he hadn't received seven more votes, the election would have been decided by the members of the House of Representatives in Washington

City. By midnight, though, it was announced that he had won New York, and with it enough electoral votes to win the presidency."

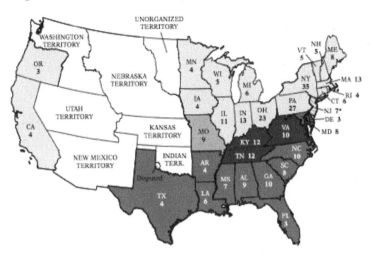

Willie Turbush raised his hand to speak. "All that electoral vote business seems complicated to me," he declared. "Why don't we just give the election to the man who gets the most votes, period?"

"Good question, Willie," Mr. Clingman said. "When the Founding Fathers devised our system, they were concerned that the people who lived in the large population centers of that time, like Boston, Philadelphia, New York City, Charleston, and Baltimore, could control presidential elections. So, they came up with the electoral vote system. Thus far, it has worked pretty well, Willie."

"Mr. Clingman," Sarah Dittman asked, "you read us an article several weeks ago that said people in the South had threatened to leave the Union if Lincoln won. Is that going to happen?"

"I remember that too, Sarah. But I don't know if that's going to happen. We'll just have to wait and see."

"When will Mr. Lincoln actually move to Washington City, Mr. Clingman?" Margaret Petzold asked.

"He will be sworn in next March, Margaret. Then he will move into the White House with his family and take President Buchanan's place. Until then, Mr. Buchanan will continue as our president."

Another student raised a hand. "What is it, Miss Drieborg?"

"Why do they wait so long for the new president to take over?"

"That is another good question, Ann," Clingman responded.

"When the Constitution was adopted seventy years ago, it took much longer to count all the votes than it does today. Remember, they didn't have the telegraph back then. Also, the roads were so poor then that it took much longer to travel; there were no railroads then. One day, swearing in of the president might be moved up and take place closer to the election. Who knows what might happen?"

Michael Drieborg was the next student to ask a question. "Yes, Mr. Drieborg."

"What will Mr. Lincoln do about slavery, Mr. Clingman?"

"During the campaign, he promised to do nothing; that is, he promised to leave it alone where it already exists. But at the same time, he and the other Republican party candidates pledged to keep slavery out of the territories and out of the Free States."

"Why is that such a problem for Southerners?" Ethan Schock asked.

"Understand, class, that when a farmer plants the same crops on the same land season after season, the soil sort of wears out. Then, the yield per acre of whatever crop the farmer is growing goes down. When that happens, the amount of that crop available to sell goes down, and so does the profit to the farmer. But the farmer's costs do not go down. So eventually, the farmer must move his operation to fresh land if he is to continue making a profit. Ask your fathers about this. They're farmers. They understand how this works.

"Those in the South who grow cotton are in that same position. The 'Cotton Kingdom,' as it is sometimes called, has moved south and west over the last fifty years in search of fresh soil and to expand production to meet increased world demand. For the same reasons, in the years to come, they will need more fresh soil and will want to expand production to meet the ever-increasing world demand.

And, of course, they would need to take their labor force of slaves with them into those new territories.

"You might remember a news article we discussed last fall. Southern leaders like Senator Jefferson Davis proposed that we take some more land from Mexico and even take Cuba from Spain, just to obtain more land for cotton production.

"So, if Lincoln's government denies them access to the unorganized territories we now have and refuses to obtain more land suitable for cotton production, they will be locked into using the land they currently cultivate.

"Continued use will eventually yield less and less cotton per acre each year. That also means that the cotton planters will not be able to keep up with the expected increase in world demand or increased cost of farming. Economic ruin and the destruction of the current way of life in the South would result.

"The other big issue is the tariff. The Republicans have promised to raise the taxes placed on many goods imported into this country. Now that they have control of Congress and the presidency, those taxes will probably be raised, thus increasing the price of imported goods.

"When that happens, the domestic and foreign-made goods Southerners need to buy will cost more. Then, too, foreigners will sell less of their goods in the United States and therefore have fewer dollars to buy Southern exports. Thus, a high tariff could be very bad for the South.

"That's why, students, many in the South threatened to leave the Union if Lincoln was elected. Well, he was elected, wasn't he? So, now we will see what happens next."

"Miss Turbush, you look puzzled. Do you have a question?"

"Yes, sir, I do," she responded. "How will economic decline in the South destroy their way of life?"

"You people are full of good questions today," Clingman responded, "but we don't have enough time left this afternoon to get into that. Remember your question and ask it again tomorrow, Mary. Will that be all right?"

"Yes, sir."

South Carolina Leaves the United States

School was out for the Christmas holiday. Michael and his father were in town on Saturday morning. As was his custom, Mike had stopped in the town's library while his father was at the grain elevator. There, Mike would pick up books his sisters wanted and one for himself; Charles Dickens was his current favorite. He also would look through copies of the *Grand Rapids Eagle* and the *Weekly Enquirer* that had accumulated since his last visit. One headline attracted his attention.

In their December 21st, 1860 edition, the *Grand Rapids Eagle* reported that delegates from across South Carolina gathered in Charleston on December 20th and voted for their state to leave the United States. A reprint of the special edition of the *Charleston Mercury* was reprinted on another page of the local paper.

On his way out the door, Mike took a free copy of the *Enquirer* to show his father.

CHARLESTON MERCURY
EXTRA

Passed unanimously at 1:15 P.M.

December 20, 1861

To Dissolve the Union between the State of South Carolina and other States united with her under the compact entitled "The Constitution of the United States of America."

We, the People of the State of South Carolina in Convention assembled, do declare and ordain, and it is hereby declared and ordered,

That the Ordinance adopted by us in Convention on the twenty-third day of May in the year of our Lord one thousand seven hundred and eighty-eight, whereby the Constitution of the United States of America was ratified, and also all Acts and parts of Acts of the General Assembly of the States, ratifying amendments of the said Constitution are hereby repealed; and that the union now subsisting between South Carolina and other States under the name of the United States of America is hereby dissolved.

THE

UNION

IS

DISSOLVED!

***

Mike joined his father at their wagon.

"Papa," he said excitedly, "did anyone at the grain elevator tell you what people in South Carolina just did?"

"Yes, I heard, Michael. One of da farmers had heard da news from Mr. Safford. A copy of his Lowell weekly paper was at da elevator, too. So, I read da article about it while I was waiting for our grain to be ground."

"What do you think, Papa?" Mike asked.

"Here, son," his father told him, "help me load dese sacks on our wagon. We can talk of politics on da way home."

"But Papa, the rest of the South may leave, too. What South Carolina did is very important."

"Dat may be, Michael. But, so is loading dese sacks on da wagon. And so far, I'm da only one doing it. We have work to do back home. Dat's important, too.

"Besides," Jake continued, "will anything we have to say change anything? I think not. But our cows will not like our being late milking dem on time. So, help me here. We talk on da way home, eh?"

"Yes, Sir."

The Drieborg farm wagon wasn't far down the road when Mike brought up the subject again.

"So, Papa," he began, "what do you think about South Carolina leaving the Union?"

Jake chuckled, looked at his son, and admitted, "When I first heard of it back in town, Michael, I must confess that I had a hard time even placing just where South Carolina is located. On da Atlantic Ocean side and south of Washington City, I think. Is dat right?"

"Pretty close, Papa," Mike told him. "Actually, North Carolina is between that state and Washington City. To the east is Tennessee, and to the south is Georgia. Our teacher told us that according to the last census, there are more Negroes in South Carolina than white people. He also told us that the farmers of that state export a lot of cotton and rice and import a lot of manufactured goods from our Northeast. They are a big user of New England-owned ships, and they use Northern banks, too."

"Thank you for all dat, Michael. Do you think dey will stop selling da cotton or rice?"

"I can't imagine them changing. Their entire economy is set up to produce agricultural goods for export. That's why the landowners have all those slaves."

"Now I have another question, son. Now dat dey live in another country, do you think da people of South Carolina will still need to buy all da things from da North, like manufactured goods, and use da North's shipping and banking like you said?"

"I would think so, Papa," Mike answered.

"Then tell me, Michael," Jake continued, "why is it so important to us if South Carolina stays in da Union?"

"I don't actually know how to answer that question, Papa."

But Mike's father wasn't done with his questions. "Now dat South Carolina is gone from da Union, do we in da North have to help da slave-owners der recover slaves who run away to da United States?"

"I wouldn't think so, Papa," Mike answered.

"So, maybe it's good for da people of South Carolina and for us, too, dat they left da Union?"

"Maybe it is, Papa," Mike admitted, "but it doesn't seem right, just the same."

"We shall see, son," Jake predicted. "We shall see."

Christmas Celebration

Snow had been falling on and off for several days. It was definitely going to be a white Christmas Eve. A full moon was high in a clear sky. The temperatures had fallen that evening, and a chilly breeze drove snow from the fields across the road.

Jake Drieborg and his sons had covered the wagon with its canvas tarp to keep out the bitter wind. Nothing would keep the Drieborgs from attending Christmas Eve Mass.

As was their custom, they arrived at their church fifteen minutes ahead of the ten o'clock starting time. For, as Jake Drieborg frequently reminded his family,

"Come everybody, da Drieborgs will never be late for church."

After the gospel reading, members of the parish reenacted the birth of Jesus. The pastor, Father Farrell, told the Christmas story to the young people who had been welcomed to the front of the church to sit with him.

When the service was over, most of those present stayed for hot cider and freshly baked bread. It was an opportunity for all to greet their neighbors and wish them a "Merry Christmas."

Rose Drieborg was talking with Joseph Deeb, the Lowell Justice of the Peace and a local lawyer.

"Merry Christmas, Mr. Deeb," she said.

"The same to you, Mrs. Drieborg," he responded. "I hope your family is well."

"Oh, yes, thank you," Rose said. She knew he was a single man with no family in the area. "Have you made plans for Christmas dinner tomorrow?"

"No, I haven't, Mrs. Drieborg. As you know, I'm a bachelor, so I planned to go to the restaurant at the Franklin House for dinner tomorrow."

"You are welcome to join us if you'd like," she told him. "The children will have us up for their presents very early. But we will not eat our Christmas dinner until noon. Would you like to join us?"

"That is most kind of you. Are you sure it wouldn't be too much trouble?"

"It's no trouble at all. We can't have you eating alone on Christmas Day when we have plenty, now can we? So, it is settled. You will join us tomorrow at about 11:30."

"That would be wonderful. Thank you, I'll be there."

Then Rose asked him, "May I call you Joseph?"

"Of course, you can. Please do."

"Then you will call me Rose. My husband Jake and I will see you tomorrow morning."

On the way home, Rose told the family that they would have a guest for Christmas dinner the next day.

Ann and her sister Susan were sitting in the back of the wagon.

Ann spoke first. "I think he's cute," she whispered to her sister.

"Don't you think he's a bit old for you?" Susan remarked.

"I don't want to be a farmer's wife, Susan," Ann responded. "He's a lawyer, and he's single. What more could a girl want?"

"How about a husband you loved?"

Ann wasn't done. "A husband who has a good career and a nice house in town is of greater value to me than getting up at five every morning to bake bread, work in a garden under a hot sun, and do all the other things a farm wife has to do while bearing and raising children. I've decided that love is a luxury I'd pass up for security and a better life."

Amazed at this outburst, Susan could only say, "Merry Christmas to you too, Ann."

"Aren't we home yet, Papa?" Little Jake whined. "I'm hungry."

"You're always hungry, squirt," Ann teased.

Jacob snapped back, "At least I'm not all skinny like you."

"Momma!" Ann complained.

"Jacob. You apologize to your sister right now, or there will be no Saint Nicholas for you, young man," his mother threatened.

"Oh, all right, Momma. I'm sorry, Ann."

"Papa," Rose continued. "I want you to have a talk with your son. Remind him, please, that Jesus said the second most important commandment is to love one another."

"You are right, Momma," Jake responded. "Ve will talk about dis cruel talk of yours in da barn. Won't we, Jacob?"

"Yes, Papa." Little Jake responded.

Christmas Day

Rose and Jake were up very early, as usual. She had bread baking, and her husband was in the barn with Mike doing the morning chores.

"Momma," Little Jake shouted from the loft where he slept. "Is it time for presents yet?"

"No, son," Rose responded. "Papa is still in the barn with Michael. But if you want to wait for them with me, I'll give you some fresh warm bread and fix you some hot chocolate. What do you say, Jacob: more sleep or food?"

"I'll be right down, Momma."

"It seems a long time since he mentioned Saint Nicholas," Rose thought. *"At twelve years old, I suppose he's too old for that now. My children are growing up so fast. I'll be losing them before I know it."*

It wasn't long before Jake and Mike came into the house.

Ann came out of her bedroom. As she pulled on her robe, she complained. "Who's making all that noise? Sounds like a herd of cattle, for heaven's sake. Do you realize we didn't get to bed before midnight, and it's only seven o'clock in the morning on Christmas Day?"

Mike laughed at her remark. "Poor Annie. Did the working men of this family disturb your beauty sleep?"

Never one to allow her brother the last word, she responded, "Let me remind you, brother dear, that you are only sixteen years old. You're hardly a working man."

"Ha, ha, ha," Mike responded, "that's very funny. I'd like to see you get up at dawn and work out in this cold for two hours. I would love to sleep in till seven one of these days."

"Breakfast is just about ready, everyone," Rose announced. "Ann, waken your sister, please."

"Can't we open presents first, Momma?" Little Jake whined.

Susan was up but not happy about it. So, she snapped, "Sit down, little boy. We're eating first. Like we always do."

"You're not my boss. So, don't go ordering me around," Jacob protested.

"Children, please! None of that kind of talk at my table," Rose ordered. "We'll open presents after the breakfast is over, Jacob. So sit down, please."

"Oh, all right, Momma."

Truth be told, all the Drieborg children wanted to open presents. So, breakfast was over very quickly.

Rose took charge of this, too.

"Jacob," she began, "you hand out the presents for me and Papa."

"But, how can I tell who they go to?" he asked.

"There is a label on each package," his mother told him, "do you see it?"

"Oh, yes. I see it now. Now, what will I do?"

"Hand one package to each of us, please," she directed. "Papa will open his present first."

"My package is very small, Momma," Jake said. "I wonder what dis gift could be." He finished taking off the wrapping.

"Oh, it's a pocket knife! Thank you, Momma. I can really use one like dis. It even has an engraving of some sort on da blade."

Jake leaned over and gave his wife a kiss.

"You're welcome, Papa. It is a special knife called 'A Minute Man.' The engraving on the blade is there to remember the first battle of the Revolutionary War, the Battle of Concord in April 1775."

"Dat is special. Thank you again," Jake repeated. "And thank you for da new slippers, too. Now, you open a gift, Momma."

She did. "Oh, look, children. Papa got me a nice new robe. It feels so soft," she passed her hand over it. "And he got me slippers, too. Thank you, Papa."

"You're welcome, Momma. "

Little Jake spoke up. "Why do all the older people get to open theirs first?"

"Because, squirt," Ann snapped.

"Just because? That's no reason."

Everyone ignored him and turned to Mike's present.

"What's in the box, Michael?" Susan asked him.

He shook the box, looked at his sister, and said, "I have no idea." So he tore off the paper covering and opened it.

"Work shoes," he announced, holding up the brand-new shoes he had taken out of the box. "I can sure use these. My toes are all scrunched up in my old ones. Thank you, Momma. Thank you, Papa. "

"You're welcome, son. Mr. White, da shoemaker, told me dat your old ones would cost almost as much to repair as to buy new ones. You got a lot of use from dat old pair, believe me."

"That's right, Papa," Mike told him. "Jacob, I'll bet you'll be happy that the old ones are too beat up to pass down for you to use."

"That's for sure, Michael," Little Jake agreed.

"Now, it's your turn, Susan," her mother told her. "See what's in your box."

She tore off the wrapping hurriedly. "Oh, look! I got a new winter coat, just what I needed. Thank you, Momma. Thank you, Papa."

"It's Ann's turn now," Little Jake announced, eager to be next.

Ann was quick to open her present. "I got a new winter coat, too. At least mine is a different color than Susan's. And now I don't have to wear her old hand-me-down coat. I've got a new one of my very own. Thank you, Momma. Thank you, Papa."

"Now, can I open my presents, please?" Little Jake begged.

"Yes, son," his mother said, "you can open yours now."

"Why do you have so many packages, Jacob?" Ann asked.

"Because I'm a kid, that's why," he said, sort of testily.

He opened the smallest gift package first. "Oh, look, Mike. I got a pocket knife, too. Just like Papa's. It's my first one."

"What else is in that stack of presents, little brother?" Susan asked.

"Hold your shirt on. I'm getting to them."

He tore the wrapping off a box that looked strangely like the one his brother had opened a few moments before.

"Work boots!" he shouted. "Just like yours, Michael. Now I have my very own boots, too. No more hand-me-downs for me. Thank you, Momma. Thank you, Papa. "

Jake told his son, "You're welcome, Jacob. But you know what dat means, don't you?"

"No, Papa. What does it mean?"

"Now you have men's boots, son. Dat means you will have to do a man's work now."

"Oh, ya."

Mike was laughing at his father's comment.

"I don't like the way you're laughing, Mike," Jacob commented.

"You'll find out soon enough, Jacob," Mike predicted.

Jake had slipped out of the room to go into the entryway. When he returned, he held a rather large box and set it down in front of his son, Jacob.

His son looked inside. "Oh my gosh! It's a dog! Is this my very own dog, Papa?"

"Yes, it is, son," Jake told him. "Now it will be up to you to take care of him, too. Do you think you can do dat?"

"Oh yes, Papa. Will you help me some? What's his name?"

"I'll help you train him, son. But you must think of a name for him yourself. After all, he is your dog."

"Where does he sleep and stuff?"

Jacob's mother spoke up at this point. "Tonight, he will sleep in the cellar. But we will talk about all of that later. For now, you can play with him in the house."

Jacob hugged the little puppy.

"What about the stockings, Momma?" Ann asked. "Do we open them now?"

"No. I think we will wait till after dinner today. I have hung one for our guest, Mr. Deeb. So, we'll wait on the stockings."

"Come now, girls," she continued, "put away your things; we have Christmas dinner to prepare. Our guest will be arriving soon."

"What about the boys, Momma?" Susan complained. "Why don't they have things to do?"

"Michael was up at dawn helping Papa while you were sleeping. I got the bread and the pies cooking then, too. Jacob has to haul in the wood for the fire and empty the chamber pot. Would you like to do that instead of helping me?"

"No, Momma."

"Momma got ya there, sister dear," Mike whispered.

"Oh, be quiet!" Susan told him.

***

Rose was right. Her guest arrived right at the time she had suggested, eleven thirty. Everyone heard a knock on the door.

Jacob ran to open it. "Hey, everyone," he shouted. "It's Mr. Deeb."

"Well, Jacob. Don't leave him outside. Invite him to come in, for heaven's sake," Ann chided.

"I was going to. Give me a chance, will you?" Jacob snapped back.

Their guest had no sooner stepped inside the entryway than Jacob was in front of him holding up his new dog.

"Do you want to hold my dog? It's a puppy, and it is my very own."

"Sure, Jacob," Mr. Deeb told him pleasantly. "But, first, let me get out of these wet shoes and my coat." He found a hook for his coat and changed into dry shoes before he entered the house.

Jake stepped forward and shook Deeb's hand. "Merry Christmas, Joseph," He said. "Welcome to our home."

"I wish the same to you, Jake. Merry Christmas, everyone," he said. "I hope you don't mind. But I put my horse in your spare stall."

"I don't mind at all, Joseph. I would have had Michael do dat for you. Did you find da water and grain for your horse?"

"No, I didn't."

Mike came up and shook his hand as well. "Merry Christmas, sir."

"The same to you, Mike."

"Son," Jake directed, "go and wipe down Mr. Deeb's horse and give him some water and grain, will you?"

"I'd be happy to, Papa."

"Where can I put these gifts, Rose?"

"Oh, my stars, Joseph!" Rose exclaimed. "Did I forget to tell you not to bother?"

"It wouldn't have made a bit of difference, Rose," Joe Deeb responded. "I would have brought each member of the family something anyway.

"It is really blowing out there now. And cold, too," Deeb told everyone. "That wind went right through me. I'll bet it's close to zero with all that wind."

Jake told him, "Have a seat by da fire, Joseph. Susan, will get you our guest some hot cider?"

"I'll get it, Papa," Ann decided.

Susan just shook her head. *"There goes Ann taking over. If she's made up her mind about him, he's as good as hers."*

He warmed his hands on the mug Ann gave him. "Oh, that feels good, just holding the mug. Thank you, Ann."

"You're welcome."

He carefully took a sip of the hot liquid. "My, that tastes good. I could have used something hot like this on the way from town."

Ann was still standing by his chair. "Where do you live in town, Mr. Deeb?"

"I have rooms at Mrs. Schultze's rooming house. Her place is at the east end of town. So, I have only a short walk to my office. She provides her roomers with breakfast and supper, too. While I would prefer a home of my own, this serves my current needs very nicely."

Ann wasn't done with her questions, though. "You said that you live alone. So, I assume you're not married?"

"Ann!" Rose snapped. "Mind your manners."

"That's all right, Rose," Deeb responded good-naturedly. "I'm sort of new in town, Ann. People don't know much about me. No, I'm not married. I'm a single fellow."

Ann continued, "Do you want to have a wife and family?"

Rose muttered under her breath, "*That girl will be the death of me, yet.*"

Jake just sat, puffed on his pipe, and listened. Mike smiled, and Susan put her hand over her mouth to hide her grin. "*That's my sister Ann. She gets right to the point.*"

"Yes, I do, Ann," he responded. "Right now, though, I'm pretty busy with my law practice and my duties as Justice of the Peace. I'm too busy to get involved in courtship, anyway.

"Besides, there aren't many eligible young ladies around Lowell. But, one of these days, I believe I'll find a lady to settle down with. Maybe you have someone in mind for me."

Ann turned away, her face having reddened some. Her father smiled.

Susan almost laughed out loud. "*He got you there, sister dear,*" She thought.

Rose retreated to the kitchen. "Come, girls. Help me here. It's time to serve the meal."

The food was soon on the table, and Mike had returned from the barn. "Come to the table, everyone," Rose directed.

Ann seated herself next to their guest.

"Susan," Rose decided, "I think it is your turn to say grace."

"Yes, Momma."

She led the prayer,

"Bless us, O' Lord, for these Thy gifts

And for what we are about to receive,

Through Thy bounty,

Through Christ, our Lord.

Amen."

"Thank you, Susan. Pass the turkey to our guest, please, Papa."

"Yes, Momma."

Everyone soon had a plate full of food — turkey, yams, mashed potatoes and gravy, crushed cranberry, peas, dinner rolls, and dressing.

"Momma," Little Jake gushed, "this is so good. I could eat this every day."

"You could eat every day, all day, squirt," Ann teased.

"I'm just a growing boy. Besides, I have to do a man's work now, don't I, Papa?"

"Yes, son, you do. Your sister is just teasing you. Are you ready for seconds yet, Jacob?"

Everyone laughed at that.

"Not yet, Papa," the boy responded, "but I will as soon as I finish this plateful."

Instead of offering pie right away, Rose had a different plan.

"Let's wait until after everyone empties their stocking before we have apple pie. Does that sound good to you, Papa?"

"Ya, Momma. Dat is fine."

"Michael, would you get the stockings hanging on the mantle?"

"Yes, Momma."

"Can I open mine first this time?" Jacob asked. "I was last this morning."

"That's fine, son. You go right ahead and empty your stocking first," Rose told her youngest.

Jacob rummaged around in the oversized stocking. He pulled out his arm, holding a dog collar. He reached in again and found a small pamphlet.

"I think the collar is for my new dog," he guessed. "But, what is this book for?"

His mother responded. "I saw that book in the catalog, so I sent for it. Those are instructions for training your new dog. The person who wrote the book tells you how to go about training the dog to obey commands like 'come' or 'fetch.' Things like that."

"You mean my dog won't just do those things?"

It was his father's turn. "I will help you some, Jacob. We'll train da dog together."

"What's in your stocking, Ann?" her mother asked.

Ann pulled her arm out of her stocking and came up with several pencils and a small notebook. "It's a diary, Momma. How did you know I wanted to start writing one?"

"Mothers know a thing or two, daughter."

Susan discovered some hair ribbons and a new hair brush. Michael found a new hairbrush, a shaving mug, and a razor.

"I've noticed some peach fuzz on your upper lip, son," his mother told him. "I asked Papa, and he said it was about time you began to shave, at least for church on Sunday."

"Shaving now. My goodness, Michael is becoming a big shot," Ann teased.

"That's no way to talk to your brother, young lady," her mother admonished.

"What did you find in your stocking, Joseph?"

"I received a package of oatmeal cookies from a secret St. Nick, thank you. I will enjoy them with my coffee at the boarding house.

"Now, it's my turn to give. I'm sorry I didn't have time to wrap them.

"I got Mr. Zania to open up his store for me this morning. I didn't know what each of you would want. But I hope you like what I chose."

He handed Jacob a small package. "I got some candy for you, Jacob. Michael, I thought some ball & powder for your hunting musket would be useful.

"I must admit I was at a loss when it came to getting something for you, girls. So I put money in an envelope for each of you to buy something for yourselves."

Susan and Ann looked into the envelopes he handed them.

"Thank you so much," Ann gushed, "I never had money of my very own to spend. What a treat."

"Jake, I set a new ax in the entryway for you, along with a box of large Mason jars for you, Rose. I wish my gifts could be less practical and more festive, but I didn't have much time this morning."

Jake thanked him. "Your gifts are from da heart, Joseph. We know dat and appreciate it. Thank you."

"Yes, we do, Joseph," Rose added. "Thank you for being so thoughtful. But how did you know I could use the canning jars?"

"I asked Mr. Zania what you could use. He suggested that gift."

"Of course. He would know, wouldn't he?"

Later in the afternoon, Jake invited their guest to help him in the barn with milking and other daily chores.

"I'd love to, Jake," Deeb responded. "But I must warn you. I'm not very skilled in such work. You might regret inviting me."

"Don't worry about it, Joseph," Jake assured him. "Michael will join us. Between da two of us helping you, I'm sure you will do just fine."

In the barn, Deeb sat at Mike's accustomed spot on the three-legged stool, milking a cow like a veteran.

"With all this milking, it is no wonder farmers have such strong arms."

"Joseph is doing pretty well milking for da first time, eh Michael?" Jake commented.

"He is, Papa.

"Can I ask you a question that has nothing to do with milking?"

"Certainly, Michael. What is it?"

"How do you think Mr. Lincoln will react to South Carolina's leaving the Union?"

"I believe he will have to treat secession as an illegal act, a rebellion against the United States."

Jake entered the conversation at this point. "If you think dat, Joseph, you must also think he must use force if dat state doesn't return to da Union."

"Yes, I do, Jake," Mr. Deeb responded without hesitation. "If he doesn't put down this rebellion, the United States as we have known it will disintegrate. Not only will other states leave whenever they choose, but the states themselves will be shattered by internal disputes.

"Things we now enjoy, like a strong currency, the protection of our navy, treaties with foreign nations, internal improvements funded by a common tariff, all could be a thing of the past.

"It would be an intolerable situation. Majority rule would not be possible. Elections would be a farce; laws made would be ignored. No, Jake, the United States would descend into anarchy. We'd probably see one state or groups of states taking advantage of others. The stronger states would absorb the small ones, just as we've seen happening in Europe for centuries.

"Our individual freedoms would be at risk, too. Our commerce would be defenseless against the navies of foreign countries. I can see the states of New England forming a union of sorts and aligning itself with Great Britain in exchange for the British navy protecting their commerce and continued access to the fishing rights we now enjoy. They might also give them access to the sugar of the Caribbean just to sweeten the deal."

Mike smiled at this little joke.

Deeb continued, "Alliances of other states with France and Spain wouldn't be far behind. Our involvement in their disputes and wars would most likely follow.

"So, I believe Mr. Lincoln cannot allow South Carolina to secede. He must do whatever is necessary to require their return to the Union, even if it means using force."

Jake and his son had remained silent throughout their guest's virtual rant.

"My goodness, Joseph," Jake finally said, "I had not realized all da possible consequences of secession."

Deeb apologized. "Excuse me. I didn't mean to get so carried away."

Mike finally said something, "So, Mr. Deeb, it's actually about the survival of majority rule, isn't it?"

"Yes, it is, Mike," Deeb agreed. "The people of the United States are the only ones on this planet who are ruled by the will of the majority. We live in the only country where people like your father and me, and other working men like us, have a say in who governs and the laws we live under. That is what is at stake."

"Wow!" Mike said.

"You have given us much to think about, Joseph. Thank you," Jake assured him. "But it is almost supper time, and we don't want to upset Momma by being late."

"I understand," Deeb said.

They washed up and returned to the house. As Jake had predicted, Rose already had leftover turkey, fixings, pie, milk, and coffee on the table.

"I was just about to send out a search party for you three," Rose said cheerfully. "Everything is ready. Jacob, it is your turn to say grace."

Shortly after supper, Joseph Deeb said his goodbyes and left for his boarding house in Lowell.

***

As the two girls got ready for bed in their room, Susan remarked on her sister's behavior.

"I'm surprised you didn't go home with our guest, the way you fell all over him this afternoon."

Ann was sitting on the bed writing in her new diary. "As I've already told you, sister dear," she reminded Susan, "I don't intend to live the life of a farmer. So what of it if I have my eye set on a better life? Joe Deeb might be the man to provide it. You just never know."

"Don't get huffy, Ann. I was just kidding you. But you only turned fourteen last November. Aren't you a bit young to have your mind made up and everything?"

"I don't think age has anything to do with it, Susan. I know what I want in life. So I might just as well take a good look right now at how I can get it."

"I guess," Susan turned out her lamp and slipped under the covers on her side of the bed. Ann left her light on because she wanted to write in her new diary.

***

Dear Diary,

Christmas Day, Dec. 25, 1860

I suppose I should introduce myself. I am Ann Drieborg. I turned fourteen last November and am a five-foot-five, light brown-haired and blue-eyed girl. Recently I noticed that I'm developing a figure. At last!

What a fine Christmas this has been. My new winter coat was very welcome, this diary was in my stocking, and some cash was received from our unexpected dinner guest. The year 1860 has almost ended. We shall see what 1861 brings. More later, Ann

***

Then she put her diary away and turned off her lamp. She snuggled up to her sister under the blankets.

"Good night, Sue. I love you."

"Good night, Ann. I love you, too."

The New Year

The first days of 1861 saw temperatures way below freezing and snow falling so thick that farmers dared leave the warmth and safety of their homes only to go to the barn at milking time. It was not surprising then that schoolchildren stayed at home. Their Christmas vacation was longer than expected.

"Michael," his father said, "come with me to da barn. I need help with a few things."

Rose cautioned him. "You be sure not to let go of the rope, Michael," his mother warned him.

Jake Drieborg had tied one end of a rope to a post by the back door of his home and the other end to a post by the barn door. You couldn't be too careful when the snow was blinding and the footing underneath was slippery.

"Yes, Momma," he responded.

Despite the blizzard which raged around them, both Jake and his son made it safely to the barn.

"While I milk da cows, son, you give da horse a good brushing. After you're done, secure a blanket over him. Check on his water, too. It is probably frozen in da bucket. We can't be too careful in dis cold."

"Yes, sir."

They were soon done. Jake covered each of the cows with a blanket and checked the covering Michael had placed over their plow horse.

"I think we're ready to go back into da house. Watch your footing, Michael," he warned, "der is probably some ice on da ground we can't see under all dis snow."

"I will, Papa. You be careful, too. Hold on to the rope. The snow is blowing so hard I can hardly see the lights in our house."

The two left the barn. Jake closed and latched the door behind them. Mike led the way, using the rope to pull himself toward the house some twenty yards away. He hadn't gone but a few steps when he heard his father cry out.

"Michael!"

Michael turned and saw Jake lying in the snow. Slowly retracing his steps, he knelt by his fallen father.

"Papa, can you stand up?"

"I think so. But you'll have to help me, son. I hit on my left side. So be careful of dat arm; it might be broken."

With the help of the taut rope, the two men stood very slowly. They stood still and caught their breath.

"You hold on to da rope, son," Jake said. "I'll hold on to you. Don't rush, Michael. Just slide your feet over da ground. If you feel a slippery spot, just stop. I'll understand and stop, too. All right, son?"

"All right, Papa," Mike responded, "I understand. Here we go."

Slowly, the pair took a step, paused, and took another.

"You all right, Papa?"

"Yes, son, I am. Slowly now, we're almost to da house."

And they were. They had covered the twenty yards from the barn in the blinding snow faster than they realized.

Inside the back door, Jake directed his son.

"Don't stop to take off our gear and barn shoes, Michael. Take me right into da house."

Inside the doorway, Jake paused. Rose sensed something and looked up.

"Papa," she almost shouted, "what happened?"

"I fell, Rose. Help me to a chair."

While she was helping her husband off with his heavy coat, hat, and mittens, he told her what had happened.

"I fell on my left arm. It might be broken, I think."

Cuts, bruises, muscle sprains, and burns of all kinds were commonplace on a farm. It seemed such things went with farming as sure as the day followed the night. So Rose was no stranger to them. She took charge immediately.

"Susan, get that old sheet I have stored by my sewing basket. You and Ann tear some long strips about two inches wide. Michael, get a bucket from under the kitchen sink and fill it with snow."

"What can I do, Momma?" Little Jake asked.

"Thank you for asking, son," she responded, more sharply than she had intended. "Just stay out of the way for now."

"No one lets me do anything around here. He's my papa too, you know."

Aware his youngest son felt left out, Jake said, "Jacob, Momma will be mad at me for getting her carpet all wet with my barn boots. But I can't get dem off alone with my sore arm. Will you help me?"

"Sure will, Papa," he said as he scurried to kneel in front of his father.

"Thank you, son," Jake said as his youngest first untied and then pulled off his boots. "Now take them in the entryway, please, and get my house shoes."

"You mean your slippers, Papa?" his son asked.

"Yes, son." He grinned, "get my slippers, please."

While Jake was dealing with this, Rose pulled off his shirt and pushed up the sleeve of his long underwear so she could examine his arm. She found the sore spot on his forearm.

"Ouch! Momma!" Jake complained. "Dat hurts."

"Stop complaining in front of the children, you big baby," she snapped. "If you had been more careful out there tonight, this wouldn't have happened. Now, sit still while I finish here."

She did not feel a break, nor had a shattered bone broken through the skin.

"I think you are lucky, Papa," Rose decided. "I don't think it is broken. But you have a bad bruise, at the very least. I'll wrap and ice the arm tonight. Maybe tomorrow we will see if it is worse than I think. "

In complete control now, she told her elder son, "Michael, you will do the milking in the morning. Little Jake, you plan to help your brother in the barn after breakfast. Papa will not be doing much for a few days."

"Dat's nonsense, Rose," Jake said. "I'll be fine in da morning."

"Papa, you listen to me. You will get out of bed tomorrow only to use the chamber pot and to eat, nothing more. That is final."

The children hadn't ever heard their mother talk like that to their father. They didn't know what to say. So they said nothing. Michael hid his face in the book he had been reading. The girls fled to their room and closed the door. Little Jake relieved the tension of the suddenly silent room when he said, "You've got one good arm, Papa. How about you and I play some checkers?"

Jake had lived long enough with his wife to know when she had the upper hand. "Dat sounds good to me, son. You set up da board."

"You won't be mad at me if I beat a crippled old man, would you, Papa?"

Michael and his parents laughed so loudly that the girls rushed out of their room to see what all the commotion was about.

"What did I say that was so funny?"

***

The storm lasted through the night. It was another day before the sky cleared. Then the sun came out, and the temperature rose some.

Only then did the Drieborg girls and Little Jake walk to school. Their brother Michael stayed home to do the chores.

"Rose," Jake complained, "there is no reason I can't at least milk da cows dis morning. My arm is still sore, but der is no pain."

"Let me take a look at your arm, Papa." She took off the wrap and probed Jake's forearm, looking him in the eyes for signs of pain.

"I can tell that you still have some pain there, Papa. But there is not much swelling. I'll wrap it again. This afternoon we'll begin to put on hot towels to pull the soreness out. We'll see about going to the barn tomorrow. Michael will do all your work again today."

Jake immediately reminded his son about the work to be done in the barn.

"Be sure to check on da plow horse, son. It is still very cold out der. But da snow has stopped, so you can put him out in da corral while you milk da cows. Dat should be enough time for him to get some exercise.

"Did the girls collect da eggs before dey left for school, Momma? Did da chamber pot get emptied and wood brought in da house last night?"

Michael answered his father. "All the chores have been done, Papa." But just so his father didn't feel he wasn't needed anymore, he added, "You have taught us well, Papa. Nothing has been forgotten."

Rose smiled at her son's thoughtfulness because she knew how important it was to her husband that he felt needed.

Lowell School

Even though the snowstorm had passed, a light breeze blew the fallen snow across the road, so the children had to be careful of falling on hidden ice or twisting an ankle on the frozen ruts of the road.

It was a relief to enter the warm school building. An hour earlier, Mr. Clingman had gotten a fire going in the pot belly stove.

As the girls took off their coats, Susan said, "Doesn't that warmth feel good, Ann?"

"Yes, but it will take more than a few minutes to warm up my hands and my feet, though. They're still frozen."

"Go closer to the stove," Susan urged. "That ought to do it quickly enough."

Both girls stood at the hot stove. Other girls joined them, including Louise Mohr.

"Mornin', girls," she said. "Why isn't Mike with you today?

Both Drieborg girls were wary of saying too much to Louise. "He had to stay home," Ann told her.

"You can give him my message, I suppose," Louise said. "Tell him I'm in a family way, and I think he's the father."

The Drieborg girls were too stunned to respond immediately. Finally, Ann took Louise by the arm and led her to a corner of the room. Susan followed, puzzled by Ann's action.

"Do you realize what this means, Susan?" Ann whispered loudly enough for both Louise and her sister to hear. "We'll finally get some help around the farm. Louise is strong. I'll bet she can handle the wood-cutting and the five AM milking, too. Isn't that wonderful, Susan?"

"What?" Louise said. "Don't your papa and your brother Mike do those things?"

"Oh no, Louise," Ann told her. "Our papa likes his strong drink at night, so he isn't able to get up early for the milking, and Michael is just plain lazy. He sleeps in, too. We have to do all those things. Why, after our momma gave birth to Little Jake, the very next morning she had to get up to do the milking and the baking, too.

"Michael stayed home today because our father fell down drunk during the storm and hurt his arm."

Susan began to get what Ann was doing, so she joined in. "Momma will probably have Louise empty the chamber pot in the morning, too. That will be a big relief for me. I hate that job the most."

Ann continued. "We'd love to have some help around our place, Louise. But you told us you took most of the boys to the barn. Even the boys have talked about it. Are you sure one of them couldn't be the father?"

"Well, maybe," Louise decided.

Susan added, "I even remember you told all the girls that Fred Turbush went to the barn with you more than once. He has older brothers, too. He says that he and his brothers do all the work at their place. He complained to me that his sisters practically do nothing but just sit around and help his momma some with the cooking. Are you sure Fred isn't the father?"

"Well, maybe," Louise agreed.

"Tell you what, Louise," Susan whispered. "Let's not tell anyone else right now. It will be our secret. You think about it, and we'll talk about it again tomorrow. Will that be all right?"

"I guess so," Louise responded.

On the walk home that afternoon, Susan and Ann discussed the situation.

"My gosh!" Ann exclaimed. "Our dumb brother sure has gotten himself in a world of trouble."

"He may have gotten the entire family in trouble as well," Susan added. "You had a good idea to frighten Louise with those stories of all the work she can expect to help us with. If I hadn't been so frightened myself at the prospect of having her around the house, I would have laughed at what you were telling her."

"Poor Fred," Susan said." I wouldn't wish Louise Mohr on anyone. You think she'll take the bait?"

"I hope she will, Ann. Let's pray she does. But we'll see. Best we not say anything at home, not even to Momma."

***

Jan. 1861

Dear Diary,

"Remember, I told you two weeks ago that Louise Mohr told Ann and me that she was expecting Michael's child? Today, I asked her if she was still sure she was pregnant. She gave me one of her ditzy answers, "I'm not sure."

"Whatever the case, she hasn't changed her behavior. She is still bragging about taking boys to the barn. If she so much as mentions Michael's name, Ann and I will shove her into a snow bank. He wouldn't break his promise to Papa, would he? Susan."

The Confederate States of America

During the first two months of 1861, citizens of six cotton states voted to follow South Carolina out of the Union. That number included Texas, Florida, Mississippi, Louisiana, Alabama, and Georgia. After they left the United States, they joined South Carolina and formed a new government, The Confederate States of America.

Back in Michigan, the students and their teacher followed these events by reading area newspapers.

"Good morning, students," Mr. Clingman said. "I have some newspaper articles for you to read this morning. While you read them, I will work with the young children on their lessons. Get to it now. Someone in each group read the articles aloud. Then I'll hear what you think."

In one group, Sarah Dittman read an article aloud from the *Grand Rapids Eagle*. In the other group, Ethan Schock read his group a different article from the *Weekly Examiner*. Both groups had copies of their own village paper, too. Articles in all the papers told about the newly formed government.

Shortly, Mr. Clingman joined his older students. "Well, everyone," he began, "who will tell me what was reported in the newspapers?"

Seven hands went up. "All right, Mr. Turbush. You can begin. What did representatives of the seven states that left the Union decide to do when they met in Montgomery, Alabama?"

"They decided to form a new government called The Confederate States of America. On the map in our newspaper, those states are the ones colored dark grey."

"Correct. Does this agreement have any resemblance to the Constitution of the United States?

"Mr. Drieborg?"

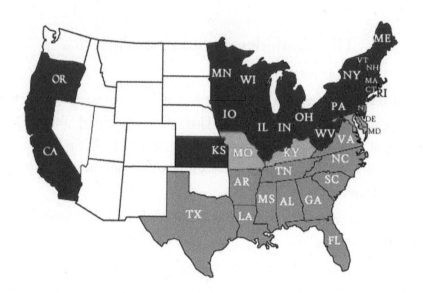

"There seem to be a lot of similarities, sir," Michael began, "but the differences are the most interesting to me."

"All right. What might those differences be?"

"For one, their Constitution recognizes slavery and the right to own slaves. They also require that member states agree they cannot leave this newly formed confederation once they join."

"As I recall," Mr. Clingman interrupted, "spokesmen for the cotton states have said for a very long time that the people of the individual states had the sovereign right to leave the Union if such membership was no longer in their best interest. So, how did this new agreement affect that right?"

"Miss Turbush?"

"It would appear, Mr. Clingman, they gave up the very sovereign power they invoked when they left the Union."

"That's correct," Clingman told her.

"But what of the big issue of slavery? Was nothing said of that in the constitution of this new confederation?" he asked.

"Miss Petzold," he continued, "what was said of Negro slavery?"

"The Confederate constitution prohibited any of their member states from interfering with a person's right to own property, including slaves."

"That's correct," he told the class.

"That's all the time we have for this morning; it's time for our noon break. This afternoon we will discuss the attempts being made in Washington to induce these states to rejoin the Union."

As part of the noon recess, the students sat at their desks and ate the food they had brought from home that day. Mr. Clingman provided a pitcher full of water for those students who didn't bring fresh milk with them.

Unless the weather prohibited it, all the students were expected to go outside when they finished. The few who came to school sick were the lone exceptions.

Actually, most of the students needed no urging. Everyone loved to get out of the building, whatever the weather, the boys especially. The girls built snowmen or stood around in groups and watched the boys. They, on the other hand, staged snowball battles or just wrestled in the snow.

The school bell signaled an end to all of that and a return to their desks. The boys returned with red faces and wet clothing from the roughhousing. The schoolroom stank from all the wet clothing.

While the students were eating, their teacher had written assignments and some information for his older students on the blackboard.

"You older students," he instructed, "read the information I've put on the board. While I'm working with the little ones, discuss what you think all that means. I'll be back to you in a few minutes.

"All right, class," Mr. Clingman began, "Miss Dittman, please read the first item I've put on the blackboard."

"Reinstate the Missouri Compromise line of 36 degrees- 30 minutes and extend it to the Pacific Ocean. And guarantee the security of slavery south of that line."

"Mr. Turbush, read the next one, please."

"Deny Congress the authority to interfere with slavery in Washington City or the Southern states."

"Miss Ann Drieborg, you read the next one."

"Compensate owners of fugitive slaves who could not be retrieved."

"These are steps some have suggested that the Congress take to get the cotton states which left the Union to return. What do you think of the first one, Mr. Drieborg?"

"You told us that when Congress passed the Kansas-Nebraska bill a few years ago, it, in effect, replaced the Missouri Compromise. Do I remember that correctly, sir?"

"Good memory, Michael. Yes, you do remember it correctly."

Mike continued. "So, just a look at the map you have on the wall shows that if Congress extended that line all the way to the Pacific, a whole lot of territory would become the Slave States, including the southern part of California. Am I seeing that correctly, sir?"

"Yes, you are," Clingman agreed.

"Sarah Dittman," he continued, "if what Michael said is allowed, which political party will have to go back on a campaign pledge?"

"The Republicans control Congress and the presidency. So, they and Mr. Lincoln will have to allow the extension of slavery into the territories and split up the Free State of California. They promised not to do either."

Mr. Clingman then asked, "Mr. Schock?"

"Yes, sir?"

"Should the Congress do this if it will bring the cotton states back into the Union?"

"Gosh, Mr. Clingman," Ethan confessed, "I don't know. Should I care?"

Mike Drieborg raised his hand. "Yes, Michael?" Clingman asked.

"My father told me that he thinks separation might be a good thing for both the United States and the new Confederacy."

"He is not alone in thinking that, Michael. I have an article from the *Atlantic Magazine* that supports that very idea. Would you like to take it home for him to read, Michael?"

"Thank you, sir," Mike responded, "I think he would like that."

Clingman concluded the discussion. It was getting dark earlier in the afternoon now, and he didn't want his students to be walking home in the dark.

"That's all we have time for today, class. Think about our discussion over the weekend. Talk with your parents about it. We'll pick up the conversation on Monday. Have a good weekend, everyone."

"You want me to clean the blackboard before I leave, Mr. Clingman?" Louise Mohr asked.

"No, thank you, Louise," he quickly responded. "You best get home before dark, so get on with you now. Thank you just the same."

While she was putting on her coat, Susan whispered to Ann, "Did you hear that? Clingman was sure quick to push Louise out the door. I think he made sure she left before the rest of us, too. I'll bet he didn't want to be caught alone with her, not even for a minute."

"I agree. If he let her stay with him after everyone else left, she'd likely say he had his way with her. That'd be his job for sure."

The Drieborg Dinner Table

Once the meal was over, the girls helped their mother with the dishes. Michael sat at the table with his father and read a geography book he had brought home from school. Little Jake was playing with his new puppy on the floor.

"When are you going to name your dog, Jacob?" his father asked.

"I did, Papa," he said. "I call him Puppy."

"What will happen when he grows up, son?" Rose asked.

"He won't know the difference, Momma. I'll still call him Puppy even when he becomes a grown-up."

Ann couldn't resist. "That is so dumb, I can't tell you, squirt."

"No one asked you anyways. Besides, it's my dog to name anything I want. Isn't that right, Papa?"

"You're right, son. If Puppy is its name, dat's what we will call it."

"See, smarty!" he sneered at Ann.

"You're not going to catch me outside calling for him to come in. Anyone who hears me will think I'm out of my mind when a full-grown dog answers my call."

"You are out of your mind," Jacob snapped.

"Enough of that talk, you two!" their mother directed, "I won't have it in my house. Do you both understand?"

"Yes, Momma," they both said almost in unison.

"How was it at school today, children?" Jake asked.

Susan remarked. "The walk to school was really cold this morning, Papa."

"It wasn't much better on the way home, either. Even with my new coat, that wind cut right through me. Brrrr!" Ann added.

Rose asked, "Tell Papa and me what you learned today, Jacob."

"Mr. Clingman said he wanted us to learn how to divide numbers. He said we first had to be able to add, subtract and multiply. So, we went over our times tables and did some other stuff on our tablets. Then he showed us how to divide."

"Show me, son," Jake said.

"Do I have to, Papa?"

"Momma," Jake said, "get a piece of paper and a pencil for Jacob. Yes, I want to see you divide."

"Oh, all right."

"We'll start with some small numbers, like twelve divided by three.

"What is da answer, son?"

"That's simple, Papa," Jacob said.

"Good. So, what is da answer?"

Jacob looked at the number twelve on his paper and the number three in back of it and drew the divide sign. Then he decided the answer was four.

"Good, son," his father said. "How about twenty-five divided by five?"

Once again, Jacob wrote down the number twenty-five and put the divide sign and the number five behind it.

"The number is five, Papa."

"That's very good, son," his mother said.

"Now for a hard one," his father warned.

"What is one-hundred-and-fifty divided by three?"

"You're right, Papa," Jacob admitted. "That is harder."

"Let me see," he wrote down the numbers on either side of the divide sign. "I think it is five, Papa."

"I think you are just guessing, son. That is not correct."

Rose stepped to the table. "How many times will three go into fifteen, Jacob?"

"That's easy, Momma. The answer is five times."

"Write that number down. Do you have any numbers of the one-hundred-fifty left over?"

"Oh, ya. I got a zero left over."

"So, what is one hundred fifty divided by three?" his father asked again.

"Fifty."

"Good, Jacob. It seems to me you're getting the hang of it. It's important dat you learn how to do your numbers. Nobody can cheat you if you can do your numbers. You will need to do it when you grow up because you won't have us to help you den. Do you understand, son?"

"Yes, Papa."

"How about you, Ann? Did you learn anything interesting today?" he asked.

"Yes, I did, Papa," she responded. "We discussed the compromises being suggested in Washington dealing with slavery."

"Why are dey doing dis, Susan?"

"Some of our leaders hope to convince the cotton state leaders that slavery will be safe in the United States forever. Then, it is hoped they will bring their states back into the Union."

Michael and Susan joined the conversation, too. The three Drieborg children told their parents the points discussed in school that day.

"I told the class that you had said it was probably a good idea for the cotton states to leave the Union," he said.

"What did Mr. Clingman say about dat, Michael?"

"He said you weren't alone in thinking that, Papa. He gave me an article for you to read that was printed in the *Atlantic Magazine*. The writer suggests pretty much the same thing you were saying."

"I would like to read dat article, Michael."

"It's in my school bag, Papa. I'll get it."

"Wait until da morning, son. Now, it's time for bed. Boys, make sure the chamber pots are empty, and der is enough wood inside for da morning."

"Jacob and I took care of those things already, Papa," Mike assured him.

"Good. All right, children. Off ta bed with ya now."

***

Dear Diary,

It is so cold, I can't believe it. On the way to school today, even my new winter coat couldn't stop the cold wind. My fingers and toes are the worst. Thank goodness Mr. Clingman has the big stove hot for us when we get to school. Ann

Behind the School House

It was well into February, and the Michigan winter gave no sign of letting up. It was cold, snowy, and windy. It was also a dreary time, too, when the sun seldom shone.

Because of the short winter days, school began later in the morning and ended earlier in the afternoon. The Lowell School Board had agreed with Mr. Clingman that it was better for the students to walk to and from school during daylight hours.

One morning, the Drieborg girls were talking with Mary Turbush during recess.

Mary asked them, "Has Louise been pestering your brother lately to meet her in the barn?"

"I talked with Michael recently," Ann said. "I asked him if he had kept his promise to stay away from her."

"What did he say?"

"He swore that he has been avoiding her."

"Well, she's been after my brother, Willie, let me tell you. Her farm is over our way, so she often walks with us. She won't leave him alone. I don't think he's given in to her. But he's so stupid about these things, he just might if she keeps asking."

Susan had an idea. "Remember when Carl Bacon would get out of hand, and the boys would take him to the back of the school to rough him up and teach him some manners?"

"Are you thinking what I'm thinking, Susan?" Mary smirked.

Sure enough, the next day during recess, the three girls had a conversation with Louise.

Ann sided up to Louise Mohr and put her arm around her waist. Mary stepped up on the opposite side, and Susan joined them from behind.

"Hey, Louise," Ann said. "I have something I wanted to show you." She and the others led Louise behind the school.

"What do you girls want?"

"At recess, I heard you asking my brother to meet you later today at your place," Mary Turbush said.

"What of it? It's none of your business, anyway."

"Oh, but it is, Louise," Mary said. "My brother may be stupid and fall for your line, but I don't. I know what you want. You want to trick some boy into marrying you. I'm sure any boy would. But it's not going to be Willie. So, if I catch you talking to him again, I'm going to knock you silly."

"That goes for us, too," Susan Drieborg warned. "You stay away from my brother Michael."

"And, while we're at it, Louise, stay away from my friend Ethan Schock, or else," Ann added.

"What do you mean, or else? Huh? Or else, what?" Louise asked defiantly.

Mary pushed a handful of snow into Louise's face. Then Ann knocked her back with a punch to the midsection. She fell to the ground. Susan stood over the fallen girl and poked her in the ribs with a stout stick.

"This is what! Huh! Huh!" Susan said as she poked Louise repeatedly with the stick. "The next time you even speak to one of these boys, we'll give you more of the same. That's what! Huh!"

By this time, Louise was crying. But she got no sympathy from her three classmates.

"Cry all you want," Mary Turbush told her. "If any of us hears that you even went near their brother Michael, my brother Willie or Ann's friend Ethan, you'll get a bunch more of the same. Got it?"

Louise said nothing.

Susan poked her again. "Did you understand what Mary just told you, Louise?"

"Yes, I understand. Leave me alone."

The three girls walked around the front of the building.

Susan was the first to speak.

"I wish we didn't have to do that to Louise. She appears to be a harmless soul. But she's determined to get a husband one way or another. I promise you, it's not going to be my brother if I can stop it. Unfortunately, we can't depend on the boys to understand the trouble she can cause them; they are so naïve."

"Stupid might be a more accurate description," Ann offered.

"That's probably true, Ann. But Susan is right, for sure. Actually, I think the three of them are stupid and naïve," Mary concluded with a chuckle. "I didn't like pushing her around either. But I'll do it again if she doesn't listen."

Ann looked at her two friends. "You know, each time I see Louise on the playground now, I'm going to say to her, 'Don't forget, Louise.'"

"Good idea, Ann. I will, too," Mary Turbush said.

"Ann, you take care of the playground. In school, I'll pass her a note each day saying the same thing," Susan told her co-conspirators. "Mary, you remind Louise when you're walking with her to and from school."

The three of them giggled.

"I think we've got it covered, ladies," Mary said.

Ann made the last comment as the sound of the school bell faded away.

"Now, all the boys have to do is stay away from Louise."

***

At home that evening, Susan sat up in bed, propped her diary against her knees, and wrote:

Dear Diary,

I never thought I would ever strike another person, but today, I did. My sister Ann, Mary Turbush, and I took Louise Mohr behind the schoolhouse. We told her to stay away from our brothers. I thought we made our demand very clear.

But she is such a dimwit; she actually pretended not to understand what we were talking about. At that point, I lost my temper and poked her with a stick three times. I wanted her to be sure she understood that we were serious. We'll see. I'll let you know what happens. Susan.

Conversation at Church

After the Sunday Mass, it was customary for most of the families to stay and share a potluck midday meal. The men would put long wood panels over saw horses with church benches on either side.

The women put the food on a table set along one wall so the meal could be served buffet style. They also set out church dishes, cups, and silverware.

Because Rose canned her garden vegetables, the other ladies expected her to bring a sampling of those. Another parishioner had been asked to bring the main dish; today, it was beef stew. Other ladies brought the rest of the meal: biscuits, applesauce, and a dessert. Milk and coffee were served, too.

It was also a weekly opportunity for sharing and conversation.

Rose leaned over to Mrs. Zania. "Mary, your cabbage rolls are delicious. Please, can I have the recipe?"

"Of course, I'd love to give it to you. I'll write it out and have it for you next Saturday when you're in town."

"Do you use any unusual ingredient I should know about?"

"Not really, Rose. I added a bit of garlic to the cabbage rolls you just ate. But I'd suggest you try fixing them without it first. Garlic can be tricky if you haven't used it much. Some of your canned tomatoes should do nicely."

"I haven't used garlic much. So, I'll take your advice and leave it out."

Mike was talking with the parish priest, Father Farrell, about the political situation.

"Did you read President Lincoln's Inaugural Address, Father?"

"Yes, I did, Michael. I was quite impressed with its mild tone. I guess I had expected him to accuse the Confederate States of treason and threaten military action against them if they didn't return to the Union. He surprised me when he did neither."

"Our teacher, Mr. Clingman, told us that his cousins in South Carolina wrote him last month that they expected Lincoln to use force against them. It appears that they were wrong."

"I hope so," Father Farrell responded.

Mike asked, "Do you think it's better if Mr. Lincoln lets the Confederate states leave the Union peacefully, Father?"

"Yes, I do, Michael," he responded. "I was assigned to a church in the Cotton South for a number of years before I came to Lowell. So, I got to know the people rather well. Quite frankly, Michael, I believe the people there are very serious about leaving the Union. If Mr. Lincoln thinks forcing them to return will be easy, he is wrong, very wrong.

"Besides, I believe the North is better off without having to contend with the slavery issue any more."

"That's what my father says, too. But there's another issue besides slavery. I read an article in yesterday's *Eagle*. It was written by a writer who works for the *Chicago Tribune*. He wrote that the Confederate Congress passed a tariff that is much lower than the one President Buchanan just signed into law a few days before Lincoln took office."

"Did the writer say why that's a problem, Michael?"

"Yes, he said that by putting a lower tariff in place, foreign goods would use Confederate ports to bring in goods instead of Northern ports. Then, because of the Confederacy's long common border with the Union, these goods would make their way into the North without the higher Union tariff and thus undersell goods produced in the North. This would then destroy our manufacturing and disrupt the entire economy of the North. He said that the economic impact would be disastrous for the North."

Mike's father joined them. "Have you two solved our nation's problems yet?" he joked.

"I'm afraid not, Jacob," Father Farrell admitted. "But I have found your son to be very well informed. If what he says is true, we are in for a rough time in the days and weeks ahead."

"I hope not, Fader," Jake told him. "Dat could mean war. Dat's something we don't need."

Father Farrell agreed. "Absolutely, Jacob, I agree. Let us pray that our leaders do not go down that road."

"Amen to dat, Fader," Jake said.

Competition, Not War, Will Change the South

It was quiet at home that afternoon. Jake sat in his rocking chair reading the *Atlantic Weekly* article Michael's teacher had sent him.

Rose was sewing, Jacob was playing by the fire with his dog, and the two girls and Mike were reading books brought home from the library.

"Listen to dis, Rose," Jake said. "Da writer of dis article is da grandson of John Adams, da second president of the United States. He says dat foreign competition will end da South's cotton monopoly and, with it, da need for slavery in America.

"He says dat already twenty-five percent of da cotton needed in England's factories does not come from our South. He also says dat amount will go up every year.

"Mr. Adams says dat in about ten years, da 'peaceful laws of trade may do the work which agitation has attempted in vain.' "

"It sounds to me," Rose suggested. "that Mr. Adams means slavery will end and the South will change without fighting a war. Is that what you think he's saying, Papa?"

"Yes, I do, Momma," Jake agreed. "I hope Mr. Lincoln and da leaders in da South listen to him."

Jacob's Toothache

It was still dark outside. Rose had gotten up to use the water closet. It was chilly in the house, and she was hurrying back to the warmth of her bed.

"Momma," she heard, "I don't feel good."

It was her son Jacob calling from his bed in the boys' loft. She went up the ladder a few rungs.

"What is it, son?"

"My tooth hurts a lot, Momma."

"Come down to the kitchen so I can look at it, Jacob."

Rose went into her bedroom for her bathrobe and slippers. Her husband was still under the covers.

"What's da matter, Momma?" Jake asked.

"Jacob has a sore tooth. I could use your help, Papa."

He joined her in the kitchen.

"Tip your head back, son," she directed. "Papa, hold the lantern up so I can see inside his mouth."

"Is it this back tooth, son?"

"Un huh, it really hurts when you touch it."

"His jaw is swollen, too, Papa. Put this hot towel against your jaw, son. Papa, get the whisky bottle for me, please." She then rubbed some of the liquid on Jacob's gum. "This might help numb the pain. We'll take him to the dentist this morning, Papa."

"Do I have to go to the dentist, Momma? The last time I went, it really hurt," he said.

"I don't know what is causing the pain, Jacob. But if something is not done, the problem may get worse. Do you want that, son?"

"I suppose not, Momma."

Instead of walking to school, the Drieborg children rode with their parents in the farm wagon. After Jake dropped off Michael, Susan, and Ann, they took Jacob to the doctor's office.

Dr. Perry, the dentist, shared a clinic with Dr. Peck, the medical doctor. The people of Lowell were fortunate to have a university-trained dentist. Such men were still scarce. Usually, the local doctor would have an assistant he trained to do dental work — to pull teeth, most often.

But Dr. Perry had been trained at the University of Michigan. When he arrived in Lowell, he spent a good deal of time speaking at churches to educate the locals on daily dental care and the need for twice-yearly cleanings in his office.

Rose Drieborg was one who listened and then insisted that every member of her family visit the dentist twice a year. Perry would scrape the tartar buildup off their teeth. Occasionally, he had to grind out a cavity-infected tooth with his hand drill, which was powered by a pulley system. After the decay was removed, the opening was filled with tin. As a result of these visits, none of the Drieborgs had lost any of their permanent teeth. Today it might be different.

Jake helped his son into the office.

"Right in here, Jake," Dr. Perry directed. "What goes here, young fella?"

"My tooth hurts."

"I put hot towels on his jaw, Doctor. I also rubbed some whisky on his gum. Neither of these things had much effect on the pain. I think he has a little fever, too; he seems quite hot, and he is perspiring."

"Before I begin, let me introduce you to Dr. Lippincott. He recently graduated from the university and is spending some time helping me before he sets up his own dental clinic in Hastings."

While he was talking, Dr. Perry washed and dried his hands. Then he lowered the back of his dental chair so that Jacob was facing up and lying parallel to the floor. There was a small stool at the side, which allowed Dr. Perry to comfortably lean over and examine his patient.

"When the body is fighting infection, Mrs. Drieborg," Perry told her, "a low fever is common. Relax, Jacob. I need to look inside your mouth; open wide, please."

After a few moments, the doctor straightened. He turned around on his stool and faced the Drieborgs. "It appears that one of Jacob's teeth is infected. We call such things an abscess. Surprisingly, he still has a couple of baby teeth. This tooth is one of them. It's in the back and should come out anyway to allow room for one of his permanent molars to come into that part of his mouth. I suggest that I pull it.

"Tell me what you think," he said to Dr. Lippincott.

Perry's colleague took the stool and looked into Jacob's mouth. "Yes, I agree with your diagnosis," he answered.

"Will that be all right with you?" Perry said to the Drieborgs.

Rose responded first, "You have told us how important it is for our children to keep their first teeth as long as possible. But if this one might cause a problem for his molar to come in, I think you should take it out. What do you think, Jake?"

"I agree with da doctor too, Rose. I think he should remove Jacob's tooth."

Jacob spoke up at this point, "Don't I get to have any say in this, Momma? After all, it is my tooth."

The adults laughed, and Dr. Perry said, "Jacob. Would you like the pain to stop?"

"Yes, I do. But it might hurt more for you to take the tooth out."

"I understand your concern, Jacob. Tell you what. I'll make you a deal. If I can take the tooth out without you feeling a thing, will you agree to let me do it?"

'You promise?"

"Yes. And your parents are witnesses to my promise. If you feel any pain, I'll give you a dollar. Do we have a deal?"

Jacob looked very solemn before he answered. "All right, Dr. Perry. We have a deal."

"I'm going to put this mask over your nose, Jacob. Your job is to breathe in deeply. Will you do that for me?"

"Is that why this won't hurt?"

"You've discovered my secret, Jacob. You're a smart boy. That's exactly why it won't hurt. Are you ready?"

"Yes, sir."

It only took a minute or two for Jacob to be under the effects of the chloroform.

"What is dat stuff, doctor?" Jake asked.

"It's something that was introduced not too long ago. People who have surgery nowadays are put under, just as I did to Jacob. It allows for surgery to be performed without the patient feeling any pain at all."

"My heavens!" Rose exclaimed. "That's wonderful."

After waiting a few minutes, Dr. Perry opened Jacob's mouth and used a plier-like tool to grasp the infected tooth. It took only the pressure of a sustained pull to extract it. Then, Perry swabbed the cavity with some sort of antiseptic, flushed out Jacob's mouth, and packed the empty space with gauze.

After he was done, he raised Jacob's chair to a sitting position. "Help me move him to the chair by that sink, will you, Jake? I'll sit by him until he comes around.

"By the way, Jake," he said. "While we're waiting, why don't you allow Dr. Lippincott to give you an oral exam? You were too busy when your family was in for theirs last fall. We have some time right now. How about it? This as good a time as any, don't you think?"

Jake hesitated.

Rose chided him. "Jake Drieborg, I don't believe it. Are you afraid to have the doctor examine your teeth?"

Shamed, Jake sat in the dental chair.

Dr. Lippincott leaned the chair back. "I'll need you to open your mouth, Mr. Drieborg." Rose turned away to hide her grin.

"Thank you. Yes, that's more like it." He used the mirror device he had strapped to his head to reflect a beam of light into Jake's mouth from the overhead gas lamp.

With a metal tool, he picked at each tooth on the upper part of Jake's mouth and then repeated the process on the lower teeth.

"You've got a good deal of plaque built up near the gums on several teeth, Mr. Drieborg. I'll need to scrape it off, or your gums might become infected, and you'll probably lose the teeth to boot."

As his examination continued, Dr. Lippincott paused. He tapped a tooth with his probe. "This tooth appears to be cracked. Do you remember when you cracked it?"

"I bit down on a pork chop maybe a month or two ago. I felt sort of a crack. But it hasn't bothered me much since den, Doctor."

"Do you feel some pain when you drink cold or hot liquid?"

"When I take a drink of cold water, I feel a sharp pain for a second or two, yes."

"I'm not surprised. The crack is so wide I can put the point of my probe into it. I believe it should come out before you get an infection there."

"Just do what is needed, doctor," Jake answered. "I want to get Jacob back home as soon as he is well enough to travel."

"I understand. Open wide, please."

"Good thing this isn't a molar. They are generally difficult to remove because of their deep roots. The tooth you cracked should have shallow roots. So, it should come out easily. I can put you out like we did your son, Mr. Drieborg, or I can just pull it out. Which would you rather have me do?"

"I'll leave dat to you, doctor. Do what you think best. I want to get my son home as soon as I can."

Little Jake regained consciousness before Doctor Lippincott was done cleaning his father's teeth.

"Jacob is awake, Mrs. Drieborg," Dr. Perry told her.

"There'll be some blood and other drainages from the extraction site for a while. So, don't be alarmed." After he squirted some water into Jacob's mouth, he told him, "Lean over the sink and spit out the water in your mouth. That's good, son. "

Then, he put some gauze in the opening where the tooth had been. "Bite down on this gauze, Jacob. The pressure will help stop the bleeding."

"How much longer before you're done, Doctor?" Jake asked.

"I'm almost done with the cleaning," Doctor Lippincott told him.

"It will be just a few more minutes, Mr. Drieborg. You've had quite a build-up on your teeth. It would be much easier on both of us if you came in for a check-up twice a year with the family. And, I must say, it doesn't look as though you brush very often, either. You really should do that once every day, you know."

"He will, Doctor," Rose assured him, "I'll see to it."

Fortunately for Jake, the cracked tooth was easily pulled. Some blood flowed from the opening until the doctor packed it with gauze and had Jake put pressure on it with his lower teeth.

***

Once at home, Jacob lay on some blankets in front of the fireplace. From time to time, his mother rinsed his mouth and had him spit out the liquid. She stopped as soon as it appeared the cavity wasn't bleeding any longer. After a good deal of discomfort, he finally fell asleep; his dog curled up at his side.

Later that afternoon, Rose heard Mike and his sisters returning from school. As they opened the outside door of the house, she rose from her rocking chair and hurried to the inside door.

"Your brother has had a rough day, and he just fell asleep. I don't want to wake him. Get yourselves a snack, girls. Then go to your room. Michael, after you get something to eat, you go to the barn. I'll call you when supper is ready."

"Yes, Momma," they answered.

It was only a few minutes, and Michael returned from the barn. "I can't find Papa," he said. "Shouldn't he be in the barn?"

"Your father is asleep in our room, Michael," she said.

"I've never known Papa to take a nap. Is he sick, Momma?"

"I think you could say that. After Jacob's tooth was extracted, your papa had his teeth cleaned. While that was being done, the dentist discovered a cracked tooth that had to be pulled. It was not comfortable for your papa, and he lost some blood, too. By the time we got home with Jacob, Papa was not feeling well either. So, he lay down. What the dentist did must have taken a lot out of your father. He's been sleeping for the past two hours."

"My gosh," Mike exclaimed. "I best get out to the barn and take care of the afternoon chores. Call me when supper is ready, Momma."

"Thank you, son. I'll send one of your sisters to get you before too long."

Lincoln Calls for Volunteers in April 1861

Just home from school, Mike burst into the barn looking for his father.

"Papa!" he shouted excitedly. "Mr. Clingman told us that yesterday, Confederate forces fired on Fort Sumter, a Union fort in the harbor of Charleston, South Carolina. He says that by doing that, the Confederate government has started a war with the United States."

Mike's father leaned against the stall he was cleaning and just shook his head.

"May God protect us, Michael," Jake exclaimed. "Such idiocy is hard for me to understand. We can only pray dat da Confederates who started dis war and our leaders in Washington will come together and find a better way dan war to solve da problems."

Mike had other news for his father, too. "Mr. Lincoln has called for volunteers to put down the rebellion, Papa. The newspaper said that there are practically no troops defending Washington City, our country's capital. So, Mr. Lincoln has called for 75,000 volunteers to enlist for three months to protect the city.

"The Confederate Secretary of War said their flag would fly over our capital in Washington by the first of May. My gosh, that's my birthday!"

"If dat would end dis war quickly, I think it would be a good idea for da Confederates to do dat, Michael."

Mike was stunned by his father's comment. But he held his tongue.

"Come, son, it is time now for da milking. We talk later, eh?"

War Talk at Home

Little Jake and Mike had come in from their chores. The prayer had been said, and everyone had filled their plates for the evening meal.

Ann spoke of it first. "Did Michael tell you about the war, Papa?"

"Yes, he did, Ann."

"What do you think of it, Papa?" Susan asked.

"It is a terrible thing, war," Jake told everyone. "You children can't imagine da killing and da devastation it brings to a country and to da people at home and to der town, too."

Despite his father's chilling response, Michael was clearly excited. "Some of the boys at school said they'll join up as soon as they find a recruiting station. They think the fight with the rebels will only last a battle or two, and they don't want to miss it," Mike told everyone.

Ann had other news. "We're going to have a party at school for them before they leave. Everyone is so excited," she added. "Just the same, I hope Ethan doesn't join up. I'd hate for him to get hurt."

Their mother spoke for the first time. "I remember when the young men from my village in France heard that Prussia had attacked our country. As I remember it, our king and theirs argued over who would be the king of Austria.

"War was declared by our leaders," she continued almost in a whisper. "Bands played in our village, and speeches were given by our town officials. The boys your age, Michael, were excited, just like you and your friends are now, and couldn't run fast enough to enlist. They didn't want to miss the fight then, either."

"What happened to them, Momma?" Jacob asked.

"Most of them never returned. We were told that disease took many before they even got to fight, some died in battle, and others were captured and perished in enemy prison camps. A few were just never heard from again. One farm boy I knew came home missing a leg, and another boy who returned couldn't hear any more. There were no bands or speeches to welcome them home, either. Their lives were shattered."

Rose stopped talking and paused. Everyone else was quiet, waiting. She took a deep breath, composing herself. "My village became a terribly sad place. It seemed as though its spirit was killed along with all our young men. It was during this time that my mother died, and we were forced to leave because of our religion. My father moved us to the Catholic part of Holland."

"Are you going to join up, Michael?" Jacob asked his older brother.

"I want to," Mike answered. "But I have to talk to Papa about it first."

Jake could see that his wife was very upset.

"That is enough talk of war, Jacob. Get the Bible, please. It will be good for us to turn our thoughts to God tonight."

***

It was very early the next morning. The light from the full moon lit the way to the Drieborg barn. As usual, Jake was in the barn doing the early chores.

"Michael," his father said, surprised. "Dis is a school day. Why are you not still sleeping?"

Mike took his place in the stall next to his father's and began milking the family's second cow.

"I can always sleep, Papa," he said. "But I can't always get a chance alone with you. I need to talk about Mr. Lincoln's call for volunteers."

"I knew dis would come," Jake thought. *"Michael wants to join up for dis war. But he needs my approval because he is underage."*

"And you want to answer his call and join up, don't you, son?"

"Yes, I do, Papa. But I need your permission because I'm not of age. Will you allow me to help defend our country?"

Jake paused before he answered. All either of the two men could hear in the silence was the hiss of the milk hitting the pail as they continued to milk the two cows.

"You know how your mother and I feel about war, Michael."

"Yes, Papa, I do. I also know how grateful you both feel for the freedoms and opportunities you have been given in this country."

"Dat is very true, son. We are thankful for da things dis country has given us. But dat does not change how we feel about war, any war. So, we will not give you permission to join."

Mike was stunned by the finality of his father's answer. Despite the chilly morning air, he felt his face flush in anger. And in his anger, he heard himself say things he never thought he would say to his father.

"Is that how you show your gratitude, Papa? Don't you feel a duty to repay this country for all it has given you? Don't you think you have a duty to help defend this country when it has been attacked?"

Rather than respond to his son's argument, Jake calmly said. "Dis is not about me, son. It is about you. You have a duty to your family, Michael. Dat comes before anything else.

"When you are of age, you can join Mr. Lincoln's army if dis war is still being fought."

Now the tone of his voice became hard. "Until dat time, you will do as I say and stay home. Do you understand what I am saying, Michael?"

Both of them had stopped their milking, and Mike was silent for the longest time.

"Michael?" Jake prodded sternly. "I asked you a question. I expect an answer."

"Yes, Papa," he said. "I will do as you say until I am of age."

Without another word, both Jake and his son resumed milking the family cows.

***

After their children had left for school, Jake and Rose sat at the dinner table with their coffee. While Jake packed fresh tobacco in his pipe, he said to his wife, "Michael wants to join Mr. Lincoln's army, Momma."

"What did you tell him?"

"I told him he would have to wait until he was of age next year."

"How did he react when you told him your decision, Papa?"

"He does not like it. He feels a deep sense of duty to our country, and it hurts him dat we will not allow him to defend it when it has been attacked. Dis is hard for him, Momma."

"It will be even harder if his friends join the army. If they are hurt or killed while he's sitting home safe, it will be even more difficult."

"Dat's right, Momma," Jake agreed. "People might think him a coward for staying home. Dat would be hard for him to take, too."

The Fishing Hole

Mike, Willie, and Ethan were at the pond. The ice was gone. May was still too early in the spring for swimming but not for fishing. So, the three friends had their poles out and their lines in the water.

"Can you believe what the girls did to Louise behind the schoolhouse?" Willie asked.

"I didn't hear this. I don't even know who the girls you're talking about are," Mike said. "Nobody tells me anything."

"My sister tells me everything," Willie revealed. "I think she believes it's her mission in life to know everything and then tell everyone what she knows."

"Do you know what he's talking about, Ethan?" Mike asked.

"I'm in the dark like you, Mike. I don't know what he's talkin' about, either."

Willie lay back against the bank with a big smile on his face.

"Now that you brought this up, buddy, you're gonna tell us what this is all about, or Ethan and I are going to throw you into the pond, clothing and all."

"I actually don't think either or both of you guys could throw me into the pond if I didn't want you to. But I'll tell you what I heard, just the same." Willie lay back again and looked up at the afternoon sun, smiling.

It was Ethan's turn to threaten now. "Come on, Willie. Out with it, or we'll just see who goes into the water."

"Ok. I'll tell ya. My sister told me that she and Mike's sisters took Louise behind the schoolhouse during the noon recess a week or so ago. Reminds me of when Carl Bacon got out of hand; we would take him back there and beat on him some. Anyway, she said they told Louise to stay away from the three of us, or they would beat her up."

"Oh, my goodness," Ethan said. "I didn't know girls did that kind a' thing."

Both Mike and Willie laughed.

"I forgot that you don't have sisters at home, Ethan," Mike said. "Believe you me, I learned long ago not to cross 'em. Cause I want a happy home."

"I'm careful too, Mike," Willie agreed. "They're tough and show no mercy when you get them angry.

"My sister told me they were just trying to protect us from Louise. They were afraid we would give in to her invitation to go with her to the barn. The girls think Louise wants to get in a family way and make one of us marry her."

"I can understand their worry, Willie," Mike said. "My sisters don't think I'd refuse if Louise asked me out to her barn again. So, it appears they took things into their own hands and are making sure Louise doesn't ask."

"Come to think of it," Ethan said. "Louise has avoided me like the plague lately. Actually, I sort of miss the time I spent in the hayloft with her. But your sisters are right. Louise is dangerous to be around. I guess I should thank them for lookin' after me."

Mike changed the subject. "Now that our sisters have protected us from ourselves, what are you guys going to do about this war? Are you going to enlist?" he asked.

The fishing poles were forgotten; the boys sat up and leaned forward with their arms on their legs.

Willie spoke first. "We talked about it at home. My older brother is going to join up next week. My papa said that if there was still a need for more troops, I could join when I turn eighteen next year. What about you, Ethan?"

"When I brought up the subject after dinner, my momma raised a big fuss," Ethan said. "I'm an only child, so I guess I understand how she probably feels. My papa thinks I'm still a kid, so he agreed with her that I should stay at home. He said it should be up to older men to put down this rebellion.

"I know he thinks this war will probably be over by the time I'm eighteen. If he's right, I'm gonna miss the whole darn thing, for sure."

Mike finally got into the conversation. "My papa said pretty much the same thing, Ethan. He and I talked about this when we were alone out in the barn before school one morning. He also said there was a reason the Army didn't want recruits younger than eighteen. It's because they want men, not boys. That comment sure got my goat, let me tell you. It was a good thing it was dark in our barn, or my papa would have seen how angry I was.

"Besides," he said, "my first duty was to my family.

"So, he won't sign for me to join. Not now, anyway. I won't be eighteen until a year from next May. If Lincoln still needs troops, I'll volunteer. But if what I read in the papers is true, the entire mess will be over by then."

"Tell me something, Drieborg," Ethan asked. "How is it that you're bigger and stronger than either of us, but you're over a year younger?"

"Maybe it's because I'm Dutch, and you're from inferior German stock."

"But I'm a faster runner than you," Ethan reminded him.

"And I'm smarter," Willy snapped.

"That'll be the day, you guys," Mike laughed.

"Whatever," Willie said for all three of them, "I guess I'm stuck here in Lowell with you two dimwits. At least for now."

"Right," Ethan agreed, "and thanks to your sisters, we can't even look forward to time with Louise in her barn anymore."

"Life can sure be hard," Willie decided.

"Hey! I got a bite," Ethan shouted and grabbed his fishing pole.

July 1861 Disaster

"Can you believe it, Papa?" Mike said. He had just returned from school, had his snack in the house, and joined his father in the barn.

"Believe what, son?"

"It's all over the news," he began to explain. "The Confederates defeated the Union Army at Bull Run yesterday. This battle was fought in Northern Virginia. Early in the battle, the Union was winning. Then the Confederates brought in troops by train from the west and hit our army by surprise in the flank. After that, according to the newspaper, our army broke apart and fled. It was a rout."

"Does dat mean da war is over, Michael?" his father asked.

"I don't know, Papa. Mr. Clingman read us the newspaper article about it. All they told the readers is that the Confederates could have walked right in and captured Washington; there was no army to prevent them."

"Why didn't dey?"

"Mr. Clingman said the Confederates were probably surprised at the Union Army collapsing and running as they did. He figured the rebels just weren't prepared to pursue the fleeing Union troops. Besides, he figured they were probably pretty beaten up and disorganized, too."

"Dat is probably true," Jake told his son. "Now, we'll see if Mr. Lincoln will end dis war and allow da Cotton South to leave da Union."

"But nothing has really changed, Papa," Mike reminded him. "The Confederates still were the ones who started this war when they attacked Fort Sumter. Mr. Lincoln said that if they were allowed to secede unchallenged, any other state could do the same, and we'd have total chaos.

"Besides, their low tariff is still a threat to the North. If the Confederate States of America is allowed to exist, so will its tariff. That would still ruin Northern industry. My bet is that the war will go on."

"We will see, Michael," Jake concluded. "We will see."

"Isn't da older Turbush boy in da Army? Was he in dis fight you just told me about, Michael?"

"Yes, he's in the Union Army," Mike told him. "I don't know if he was involved in this battle. Willie or his sister Mary will tell us as soon as their family hears."

"The reports Mr. Clingman read us in school were sort of sketchy. But it was obvious to reporters that our men gave up during this battle; they stopped fighting and ran from the field. They didn't even take their weapons with them. So, what's left of our army right now is without rifles and supplies, too. It appears to be quite a mess."

The Center of Attention

The Lowell area was agricultural. The townspeople served the needs of the farmers. Everyone depended upon a good harvest. This year, as summer gave way to fall, hay and wheat had been harvested as always, and one could almost watch the corn grow. Some farmers, like Jake Drieborg, had begun raising sheep, too. As their flocks grew, they looked forward to taking advantage of the growing market for wool.

Actually, prices for every commodity had risen beyond the expectations of even the most optimistic farmer. Market prices for wheat, corn, butter, and wool had almost doubled since the war began. If the war continued, the demand for these commodities would increase, and so would prices. That was great news for farmers.

Not so great was the fact that most families in the area had sons, relatives, or friends at risk in the Army. So, as pleased as they were with the sudden prosperity, they were depressed and frightened about the war that had given them prosperity.

The initial expectation that the overwhelming strength of the Union would make for a short war had not been realized. Instead, the battle of Bull Run in July 1861 had begun a continual barrage of bad news for the Union.

In response, Lincoln relieved the general who had been in charge of Union forces at Bull Run. In his place, he put General George McClellan and gave him the responsibility for rebuilding the Union Army and directing all aspects of the war. As a result, expectations of success were high in the North for the 1862 spring campaigns.

***

"Did either of you guys see the article in the *Eagle* about McClellan?" Mike asked.

The boys were at the fishing hole. It was a nice fall day, but they'd been here in foul weather, too. The only thing that would keep them away was chores at home.

"Who has time to read papers?" Willie taunted. "Besides, Clingman will tell us anything important. No need to spend time in the town library trying to read all that fine print in a newspaper."

Ethan spoke up. "Now that you know neither of us read the article you're talking about, what about it?"

Mike laughed at his friends.

"What's so funny, Drieborg?" Ethan asked.

"You're supposed to be so smart, Willie. Isn't that what you told us; you said you were the brains of this outfit. A person would think you'd be on top of the latest information."

"Ha, Ha, Ha! Drieborg," Willie snapped, "I'm on top of it. I already know about McClellan. For your information, my brother wrote us all about him. The troops think he is the greatest. He's putting together a huge army with the best equipment in the world. The Rebs don't stand a chance against him. In the spring, he'll capture Richmond, for sure. So, how's that for not reading your old newspaper?"

"Pretty good, I must say," Mike conceded. "I hope this army he's putting together will do that and put an end to this war."

"I hope he doesn't, actually," Ethan said.

"I'd like to join McClellan's outfit and have a hand in whipping the Rebs, wouldn't you, Willie?"

"When I turn eighteen next fall, I'm joining. Whether I'm assigned to McClellan's army or not, I'm joining for sure."

"Why don't you two wait until I'm eighteen? Then we three can join together."

"Wait until almost June?" Willie exclaimed. "Everyone says McClellan will end this thing by then. So, I'm not waiting 'till then, Mike, no way."

"Me neither, Mike. I'm sorry. But Willie's right. Can't you talk your pa into signing a few months early for you?"

"Look, guys," Mike explained for the tenth time, "I promised my father that I'd wait until I turned eighteen before I joined. I have to keep that promise. I have no choice anyway because I know my father won't sign. You two have a choice. You can wait a couple of months so we three can join together, or you can go off without me.

"Are you telling me that my two best friends in the world are choosing to leave me alone in Lowell while they go off and have a great adventure?"

"That's about the size of it, Drieborg," Ethan said. "Willie and I can't help it if you're just a kid. Remember, the Union Army only wants men."

Mike jumped up, grabbed Ethan by the front of his overalls, and threw him into the pond.

Willie was immediately on guard. "No, you don't, Drieborg. I'm not as easy as Ethan. 'Sides, I didn't call you a kid."

Just the same, Mike plowed into Willie and knocked him over. They wrestled and rolled over a couple of times until they dropped off the nearby ledge and into the pond.

All three boys stood in the shallow water, sputtering and splashing each other. Ethan and Willie teamed up against Mike and dragged him under before they returned to the shore.

"How am I going to explain these wet clothes to my mother?" Ethan whined.

"Just tell her you insulted your best friend, and he threw you into the pond," Mike suggested.

Willie rolled on the ground, laughing.

***

Mike's water-soaked shoes still swished with each step as he walked into the barn. His brother was playing with his dog.

"Jacob," Mike said, "I need a favor. Please go up in the loft and get some dry clothing for me. Get me underwear, socks, pants and a shirt. Would you?"

"What's it worth to you, Mike?" Jacob teased.

"How about I not beat on you?"

"You'd get in real trouble with Momma if you did. And you still wouldn't have dry clothes. You can come up with something better than that."

"How about I empty the chamber pot for you tonight after supper?"

"Now we're getting somewhere; how about emptying it tonight and tomorrow morning?"

Mike was wet and cold. He was also becoming irritated with his brother. "All right, Jacob. I'll do it tonight and in the morning, too. Now get my things. The sun's gone down, and I'm freezing here."

When Mike finally came into the house, Ann and Susan were setting the table. His father was sitting in his rocker smoking his pipe. His mother was filling the serving dishes. He soon discovered that everyone knew what had happened.

"Went for a swim, did you?" Ann teased. "Or did your two buddies gang up on their big strong friend and toss you in?"

Mike saw his mother looking at him with sort of a question on her face.

"Well, if you must know, Miss Busybody, the three of us were just horsing around. And before we realized it, we stumbled off the ledge and fell into the pond."

"Hear dat, Momma?" Mike's father said. "And, dese are da boys who think dey can save dis country."

Mike's sisters giggled; his mother just smiled.

Jacob was sitting on the floor, playing with his puppy. Mike gave him a push with his foot. "Thanks, big mouth."

A Promise Kept

"Com'on Drieborg," Willie urged. "Talk to your father. Ethan and I joined up already. We're going on the train to Chicago with a whole bunch of guys in a few weeks."

"Ya, Mike," Ethan said, "we can't leave you here alone. You gotta go with us."

"We've had this conversation before, guys," Mike reminded them. "I would like nothing better than to go with you. But I promised my father I'd wait until I'm eighteen."

"You are sure a stubborn one, Drieborg," Ethan concluded.

"So's my father. Guess it's the Dutch in us."

"I guess," Willie agreed. "One of us will write and tell you where we are and all that. Maybe you can join us this summer."

"I'll sure as heck try."

Before the first of November, Mike's friends were off to the war. Willie was assigned to Grant's army, fighting in Tennessee; Ethan was sent to McClellan's Army of the Potomac, getting ready to assault Richmond.

Mike followed the war in the newspaper at home.

***

Dear Diary,

Michael wants to join the Army with his friends, and Papa says he must wait until he is eighteen. My brother is so upset. I know he is no coward and is staying home only until he is of age to join. Some kids at school say he is a coward — behind his back, of course. My sister and I pray for Willie and Ethan every day. More later. Ann

***

A few weeks later, Mike received a letter from Willie. He wanted to be alone when he read it, so he stuffed it in his winter coat pocket. As soon as he finished his Saturday afternoon chores, he went to the pond.

Hi Mike,

I don't have much time, but I wanted to say hello. I can't believe how warm the weather is in Tennessee. No snow at all. They don't have much of a winter. Pretty wet and chilly, though. Still, there is a lot of sickness in our camp. It seems like there's a long line of men at sick call every morning. We don't know if they are sick or are what we call 'slackers' trying to get out of duty. Many get sick because they don't clean their mess gear very well. We call what they get, 'the shits.' Men around here have died from that. We drill a lot. I'm pretty good with my muzzleloader. I can get off two shots a minute and hit what I aim at. The city boys are pretty useless; they couldn't hit the broad side of a barn, much less a small target. They have trouble even loading their muskets. I'm a corporal now 'cause I teach men how to load and fire their weapons. Gotta go — meal time. Miss you, buddy. Willie

Mike just sat on the snow-covered bank, thinking of his friends. He watched as a rabbit scurried about.

"Get back into your hole, little fella," he thought. *"We've got a bunch of foxes around here. They'd love to have you for dinner.*

"Damn, I miss you guys. Now that I know where at least one of them is, I'll write a letter tomorrow. Look after them, Lord."

***

That next Monday, Mike was in school, telling some of his classmates of Willie's letter. He passed out slips of paper with his friends' addresses on them.

"Write him. I know he would like to hear from you," Mike promised.

"Easy to say when you are here safe and sound at home. Don't you think, Michael?" Sarah Dittman said sharply. "Shouldn't you be fighting for your country like he is?"

"Why would you make such a remark, Sarah? You know I would be right by Willie's side if I was old enough to join the Army. I will be with him as soon as I turn eighteen."

"Just seems strange to me that a grown man like you sits home and lets his best friend go to war without him. You're taller and stronger than either Willie or Ethan, yet you sit at home. Seems strange that you wouldn't find a way. That's all I mean."

Mike was fuming. *"She's suggesting that I prefer to stay home over fighting for my country. She's even saying that I'm a coward. If she thinks that, what must other people in town think?"*

"I just think you should have done whatever it took to join them, even lying about your age. Are you telling me that you couldn't have joined if you really had wanted to?"

"My friends joined as soon as they turned eighteen, Sarah. And I'll do the same as soon as I turn eighteen."

Sarah walked away from the group around Mike. "Just seems strange."

Lost Friends

General Grant's army was trying to gain control of Tennessee for the Union. At a place called Shiloh, a major battle took place in April 1862. Here, the Union Army lost more men than in any battle since the year-old war began.

Unfortunately, one of those killed was Mike's close friend, Willie Turbush. Mary Turbush brought the sad news to school. Everyone was upset. Mike just got up and left the building, sobbing. The Drieborg girls hugged and cried with their friend Mary.

Before they left to walk her home, Susan told her brother Jacob, "When you get home, tell Momma about Willie and that Ann and I will be at the Turbush house with Mary."

Mike went to the fishing hole. Both of his friends had joined Lincoln's army as soon as they turned eighteen. Ethan had been reported missing in action back in March. Now, in April, Willie was reported killed. Mike sat on the same bank where the three of them had so often talked and fished.

Images of them and bits of their conversations ran through his mind. *"This place will never be the same,"* Mike thought." *How could you allow this to happen, Lord? So many were killed! First, Ethan is gone, who knows where; and now Willie's killed. Shit!*

"Poppa's probably right. If this is the cost of keeping the Cotton States in the Union, we're better off letting the damn slavers have their own country."

Then, he had a startling thought.

"If the Union isn't fighting this war to free the slaves, is it really about the threat of financial ruin, the tariff, and all that? Did Willie die to protect the factory owners of New England or the merchants and bankers of New York?"

Mike looked up with a start when he saw his father and his brother, Jacob approaching.

"Papa?"

"I thought I'd find you here, son. Mind if we join you?"

"Not at all, sir."

"Jacob came home from school and told us about Willie. It's terrible news. Momma went over to der house with some stew she was cooking for our supper. I think Susan and Ann are already der with Willie's sister, Mary."

"It's just not fair, Papa," Mike told his father. Tears were streaming down his face. "Why did God let Willie die?"

"I don't think God did, son. I couldn't believe in a God who decides to have a war or who decides who is to live and who is to die. I rather think dat our God allows men to have wars and kill one another.

"God gave people da freedom to choose good or bad. When we choose da bad, we suffer, like now. Dat's the price we humans pay for da freedom God gives us."

"Why does it hurt so much, Papa?" Mike asked.

"It hurts because you lost your best friend, Michael."

"I suppose that's it," Mike decided. "It was bad enough when I heard last month that Ethan was missing in action. At least there is hope he's still alive. He could be a prisoner, maybe. But knowing that Willie is dead is so final. I can't get my mind around it, Papa."

"Don't try, son. You can do nothing to change it, so you must accept it.

"Can I make a suggestion?"

"What, Papa?"

"You should thank God for the time you three had together. You will have friends yet in life, Michael. But you will never have two friends like Willie and Ethan. It was a special and wonderful time for you dat will never be repeated with anyone else, I think."

"Living without them will be hard, Papa."

"Yes, I expect it will. But you must go on with your life, son. It will be hard, but you must do it."

"I'll try, Papa. I'll try."

"Come, Michael. We have work to do at home. Dat will be better for you dan sitting here alone."

***

In town the following week, Jake got news from Carl Schock about his son, Ethan.

"We just received word from the Army that Ethan is a prisoner at Belle Island Prison in Richmond, Virginia. We were given an address where we can send packages to him."

"Will da Rebs deliver what you send him?" Jake asked.

"We don't know," Carl answered. "The Army people told us that they believe the reb guards steal a lot of the packages sent to Union prisoners. We decided to send warm clothing and stuff anyway, just on the chance that Ethan would get it."

Back at home, Jake gave the news to his son. "Here is da address da Army gave da Schocks to use when dey write Ethan. Maybe we should put together a package for him, too. What do you think, son?"

"It's great to finally know that Ethan is alive. I'll write him yet today. Momma and the girls will help us get some things together for him, don't you think, Papa?"

"I think so, son. Let's ask."

***

"Come, hurry, everybody," Rose Drieborg urged. "We don't want to be late for the memorial service."

The Turbush family was having a service for their son Willie. They had been notified by the Army that during and after the battle of Shiloh, fierce fires swept the battlefield where their son was killed. This made it impossible to identify him from the other soldiers who had died on that field.

Willie, then, was buried in a mass grave with hundreds of other unidentified Union soldiers. So there would be no body or coffin to bury in Lowell, but there would be a headstone for their son in Lowell's Lutheran cemetery.

All the students from the Lowell school attended the service, along with their teacher, Mr. Clingman. Susan and Ann were with Mary Turbush, one of the girls on either side holding Mary's arms. Mike and Jacob joined their parents in the pew behind the rest of the Turbush family.

"Dearly beloved," began the minister, "we are gathered here today to honor the memory of William Turbush. We remember him as a fine young man, a credit to his family, to this community, and to the Union. He gave his life in a heroic effort to suppress the rebellion that threatened to dismember it. I have a letter from his company commander I would like to read."

"*Dear Mr. and Mrs. Turbush,*

By now, you know of your son Willie's death. What you might not know is that he was a fine soldier. He was not in camp long when I realized he was a natural leader, and I promoted him to the rank of corporal. Very quickly, the men of his squad learned they could depend upon him, too. I assure you it is a great loss for them. May God bless you and your family.

Sincerely,

Captain Robert Smith"

By the time the minister finished reading the letter, everyone was crying, even young Jacob. Michael stood ramrod straight, his hands gripped tightly on the back of the pew in front of him. He cried without shame; tears were streaming down his face.

The church choir sang a popular song of the day, "*Just Before the Battle, Mother.*"

"*Farewell, Mother, you may never*

Press me to your heart again

But oh, you'll not forget me, Mother

If I'm numbered with the slain."

The minister then led the congregation to the church cemetery. They gathered around the headstone, which read:

William Turbush

1844-1862

Beloved Son and Soldier

A three-foot staff flying a small United States flag with thirty- three stars was planted in the ground at the side of the stone. The minister concluded the service with a final prayer.

"Dear Lord, welcome our son William into your heavenly kingdom. And may his soul and all the souls of the faithful departed rest in your peace. Amen."

Then, he invited everyone to join the Turbush family in the church hall for refreshments that the church ladies had prepared.

But Mike stayed behind at the grave.

"Oh, my dear friend. How I miss you. Now that you are with the Lord, I ask you to look after Ethan. Be his guardian angel, Willie, and bring him home to us."

Lowell

It was a summer Saturday morning, and Jake was headed to town. Mike and Susan were with him. As usual, the town was crowded despite the early hour. He had to stop at the blacksmith's shop and have some grain ground at the elevator.

Mike and his sister were sent to the general store. That store was crowded, too. Like their father, they were told it would be a while until their mother's order would be ready.

Mike and Susan walked out of the store and headed to the library.

"My goodness!" Susan exclaimed. She gripped her brother's arm and pointed. "Do you see that man in a military uniform? I can't believe it, but I think it's Carl Bacon."

"Yep, I think you're right, Susan. That's our old classmate Carl, all right."

Carl was quite a sight in his Union officer's uniform. He wore highly polished knee-high boots and a wide-brimmed blue cavalrymen's hat decorated with a bright yellow feather. Not more than five-feet-three inches tall, he could not have carried more than one hundred pounds on his slender frame.

The Drieborg children stood on the wooden sidewalk with other bystanders and watched the performance Carl was putting on for the benefit of several boys who had nothing better to do than to watch this strange little man show off his new uniform.

"I thought he was at the University of Michigan in Ann Arbor," Susan said.

"He was," Mike told her. "Word is that he was expelled for cheating, drunken behavior, and poor attendance. Then, I heard that his father had purchased an Army commission for him in that cavalry regiment being formed this fall in Grand Rapids."

As Mike and Susan continued to watch, one of the kids in the audience laughed at Carl's strutting. Angry at the ridicule, Carl grabbed the kid by the shirt and began shaking him. Then, right in front of his audience, Carl raised his riding crop and hit the little boy.

Still holding her brother's arm, Susan could feel him tense up and begin to pull away from her grip.

"Oh, my. Michael's going after Carl," she thought.

"Don't, Michael," She pulled him back to her side, "you'll only cause trouble."

"That arrogant little shit's going to hit that kid with a riding crop," Mike said.

"And this is none of our business, Michael," Susan reminded him, holding her brother even tighter.

Mike pulled away from her grasp and moved quickly toward Bacon. Stepping up to him from behind, Mike grabbed the riding crop from Carl's upraised arm. "That's enough of that, Carl."

Surprised, Carl released the youngster. He turned to face the intruder. "Not this time, Drieborg. I'm an officer in the Union cavalry now," he spat with hate in his eyes.

"That may be," Mike replied, "it still doesn't give you the right to push others around."

Facing Mike, Carl had both hands on his hips. His composure restored, he retorted. "Not much you can do about it, farm boy. This uniform gives me all kinds of rights. Come to think of it, most of us in this town are doing our duty and defending our country against slavers. Maybe you're one of those Copperhead traitors who would like to see this country destroyed. Is that it, Drieborg?"

A dozen or more adults had joined the youngsters, listening to the exchange.

Mike's face was red with anger. "Watch what you say, little man." He snapped. His hands tightened into fists at his sides.

"Lookee here, everyone," Bacon said, turning to the kids and the gathering crowd of adults on the sidewalk. He pointed at Mike. "Look at Lowell's rebel lover and a real-live coward."

By this time, Susan was standing at Mike's side, holding his right arm.

He pulled away from her.

"Please, Michael!" she said, but it was too late.

Mike jumped forward, enraged. He grabbed Carl by his wool jacket and lifted him off the sidewalk as though he didn't weigh a pound. Mike walked him backward toward the street.

Carl gripped Mike's wrist and tried to kick him with his polished boots. Stumbling backward, Carl turned his head. He could see that Mike was moving him toward the water-filled horse trough by the side of the road.

"Cool off, Lieutenant," Mike ordered. With that, he dunked Carl into the trough to the cheers of the kids and the laughter of the adults who had witnessed the entire episode. Each time Carl pulled his head above the cold water, Mike pushed him under again.

"That will be enough, Michael," Mr. Zania ordered. He had heard the cheering of the youngsters gathered outside his store and had left the store to investigate. "Let him up, Michael, and go about your business. Go on, you kids. The entertainment is over."

Mike left Carl sitting on the edge of the water trough, soaking wet, catching his breath and sputtering.

Susan was again at Mike's side, pulling him away from Bacon and across the street toward the town's library.

Behind them, they heard Carl shout, "I'll get you for this, Drieborg. You haven't seen the last of me. Just you wait."

"Michael," Susan said, chuckling, "it was really funny watching Carl flaying his arms around and sputtering each time you dunked him. All the adults on the sidewalk couldn't help but laugh, too."

Mike was still angry. "Can you imagine that arrogant runt beating on a little kid with a riding crop? There were a bunch of adults watching. Why didn't one of them step up and stop Carl?"

"I wish one of them had, Michael. You still seem angry. I think you could use a dunk in that cold water yourself, brother." Her laughter did not calm him down, not one bit.

"Very funny," Mike shot back, "I don't need your humor right now."

"Maybe not," she replied, "but you need to be much calmer when Papa hears of this. You know you're in trouble with him."

"I probably am," Mike admitted. "I shouldn't have lost my temper, either. But Carl really got to me with that coward business. Others around here probably think the same. I can handle their opinion. But coming from that little bully, I lost my temper."

A bit later, Mike sat at the reading table in the single-room Lowell Library. He was reading the latest war news reported in the *Grand Rapids Eagle*. Susan was checking out several books for herself and her sister.

The Lowell Marshal, Mr. Chapman, entered the building. He looked around and then headed directly for the table where Mike sat. He stopped there and paused. Mike stood up as soon as he noticed the marshal.

"Good morning, Marshal," Mike said.

Without hesitation, Chapman asked, "Did you push Carl Bacon into the horse trough this morning?"

"Yes, sir. I did. He was beating a little kid with a riding crop, and I stopped him."

"Witnesses have attested to that, Mike. But others have said you attacked him only after he called you a rebel sympathizer and a coward. Is that true, too?"

"Yes, sir. It is."

"Well, son. Carl's father told me he intends to file assault charges against you with the Justice of the Peace. You'll have to come with me. Where would your father be about now? He'll need to know of this situation."

"I expect he will be at the elevator or at Zania's store right about now."

Marshal Chapman was the closest thing a Michigan small town had to law enforcement. He handled arrests, and the Justice of the Peace took care of hearing minor cases. More serious breaches of the law were referred to the sheriff at the county seat. In this case, that would be in the nearby city of Grand Rapids. The charge against Michael Drieborg did not call for a referral to the sheriff's office.

Susan collected her books, Mike put away the newspaper he had been reading, and all three left the library. Marshal Chapman walked a few feet ahead and heard Mike talking to no one in particular.

"For beating on a little kid, you'd think Carl would be the one arrested. Not me for stopping him."

Chapman stopped, turned, and walked back to Mike. "I would arrest Carl, but the parents of the boy he was hitting with his riding crop refused to file charges. I asked them.

"They probably fear what Carl's father would do to them. He could call in their farm loan. Ruin them, probably. And if they don't have a loan from the bank right now, they might need one in the future. No one in this town I can think of will cross that banker. That's something you might have thought of, too, young fella, before you let your temper dictate your actions."

He left Mike standing in the street and headed for his office.

Mike stood there and hung his head, stunned by the marshal's comments. It dawned on him that he had made a major mistake this morning. Furthermore, he realized that his family might very well have to pay for his foolishness.

Jake Drieborg had just pulled up to the general store. He had begun to load the supplies onto his farm wagon.

Mike approached his father and told him that the marshal wanted to see them in the office of the Justice of the Peace.

"Why would Marshal Chapman want to see us in Mr. Deeb's office?"

"Because Papa. I got into a fight with Carl Bacon."

Mike expected his father to react with anger. Instead, Jake looked at his son with surprise, as if he had been slapped in the face. He turned away from Mike, put his hands on the sideboard of the wagon, and hung his head.

In a few moments, he turned around. Mike could see that the look on his father's face wasn't one of anger, just disappointment. He looked directly at his son, put his hands on his hips, and shook his head. "Come on," he said, "we go to see Mr. Deeb and da marshal about dis, now."

In the office of the Justice of the Peace, the three Drieborgs sat in straight-backed wooden chairs in front of Mr. Deeb's desk.

Deeb looked directly at Jake, ignoring Mike and Susan. "Thank you for coming here so quickly, Jake," he said. "Mr. Bacon just left my office. On behalf of his son, he filed charges of assault against your son, Michael. Marshal Chapman has investigated the situation and will tell you what he believes happened."

The marshal then related the events of the morning. When he finished, Jake turned to his son.

"Is what da marshal said true, Michael?"

"Yes, sir, it is. But I just stopped Carl from beating on this little kid."

The marshal continued. "Mr. Drieborg, I can understand Mike's reaction to Bacon's bullying of children. But he and Carl are not kids having a schoolyard disagreement any longer. Your son can't just take things into his own hands, however justified he believed it to be. He should have called me."

The Justice of the Peace interrupted. "Harvey Bacon wasted no time after the incident to file formal charges. He just told me he intends to see to it that the law is enforced. There are plenty of witnesses. Mike himself admits to attacking Carl. We have a nasty situation here, Jake."

Mike's mind was racing. *"They're talking about me as if I'm not even here, as if I have no part in the matter. I feel bad enough about what Mr. Chapman told me out in the street. But now, I could be going to jail for assault. What was I thinking? I wasn't. Instead, I allowed my temper and arrogance to rule my head."*

"Mr. Deeb," Jake began, "you have known my wife and me for some time. We work hard and pay our debts. You have had no trouble with da Drieborgs. Dat Bacon kid has been a pain to da people of Lowell since he was old enough to walk and talk."

"All that is true, Jake. But charges have been filed," Deeb reminded him.

"How about I take care of Michael in my own way, at home," Jake suggested. "You can have my word on it. Will dat take care of dis business?"

"Not this time, Jake. I have little choice. Your son is guilty of assault by his own admission. He attacked Carl Bacon in front of nearly the whole town on a Saturday morning. Harvey Bacon already told me he would not drop those charges for any reason.

"But I'll tell you what I can do. First, Mike has to plead guilty. Then I will release him to you until Monday. Then you have him back here by eight that morning when my court opens. At that time, I will accept his plea of guilty and give him the choice of spending thirty days in the Kent County Jail or paying a one hundred dollar fine."

"Go to jail!" Mike exclaimed, rising from his chair.

"Michael, sit down and be quiet!" his father directed. "Right now, Michael!"

Mike had never known his father to speak to him with such force. His father was virtually shaking as he stared Mike into silence.

Mike sat with a thud and slumped forward, looking at the straw hat in his hands.

"But because of the war, I can offer one other alternative," Deeb continued. "Mike can volunteer for service in the Union Army. If he joins the cavalry regiment now being formed in Grand Rapids, there will be no jail time or fine."

"But Mr. Deeb," Jake asked, "isn't dat da Army unit where Harvey Bacon bought his son a commission?"

"Yes, it is, Jake. But that's the best I can do for you. Think it over. I'll see you Monday morning at eight o'clock when I open my courtroom. You can give me your decision then."

Michael's Decision

As the Drieborgs left the office of Lowell's Justice of the Peace, Jake turned to his son. "Michael," he directed, "you sit in da back of da wagon. Susan, you ride on da bench with me."

Mike looked at his father and, for the first time, saw the anger on his face.

Jake snapped the reins, and the horse began to walk home. "Michael, tell me everything dat happened," Jake ordered.

Mike told him everything in detail.

"Susan, you watched dis entire thing, yes?" her father asked.

"Yes, I did, Papa."

"So! You tell me everything you saw and heard. Leave nothing out."

When she finished, Jake said to Mike, "So! You did not dump Bacon in da horse trough because he had hit da little boy. You attacked him because you lost your temper when he called you a coward. Isn't dat right, Michael?"

"Yes, Papa, it is."

"I thought so," he concluded. "Neither of you talk now."

The remainder of the trip home seemed to take forever for Mike.

When at last Jake directed the wagon off Fulton Street and into their farmyard, he told his daughter. "Do not say anything to Momma just yet, Susan. I will decide when."

"Yes, Papa."

Mike watched Susan go into the house and his father move around the back of the wagon.

"We are late getting home, Michael. Momma will have dinner ready. Help me now."

"Yes, Papa."

They each took a sack of flour into the root cellar under the house. The ground corn went into the storage box in the barn. Mike carried the box of cooking supplies into the house. He avoided his mother's gaze and swiftly left for the barn to help his father unhitch the horse and get it settled with a rubdown, water, and grain.

When the two of them finished, they washed before going into the house for dinner, the noon meal.

All the Drieborgs were at the dinner table with heads bowed as Jake thanked God for his blessings. Then his wife began passing the plates of food.

Mike considered his mother very pretty, especially when she pulled her long blonde hair into a bun behind her head. Her bright blue eyes virtually sparked, except when she was upset with him or one of the other children. He believed she could be tougher than his father at times. He feared this would be one of those times.

She passed a dish of freshly baked biscuits, hot from the oven, and another of beef stew. Everyone loved her stew over biscuits. Applesauce, milk, and apple pie were on the table, too.

Once the food was passed and everyone's plate was full, she spoke. "So, tell me the news from town."

Jake immediately spoke first. "Michael got arrested by da marshal today."

"What do you mean, arrested, Papa?" she asked in amazement. "Arrested for what?"

Mike and Susan sat silent. Ann and Jacob excitedly asked questions.

"Be quiet, everyone," Jake interrupted. "Let Michael tell you."

Mike told them what had happened and the decision of the Justice of the Peace.

"What are we going to do, Papa?" Rose asked.

Without hesitation, Jake responded, "We have no choice, Momma. We must pay da fine."

If Mike had any objection to his father's decision, now was the time for him to say so.

"No, Papa," he said. "I intend to volunteer. You and I have talked about my joining the Union Army when I came of age. Well, I'm of age. It's time I got into this war, anyway."

The other members of the family sat in stunned silence.

I know that none of us children have ever dared to disagree with either of our parents, especially not our father. But I have to tell them that I will leave our farm and go off to war against their wishes.

"Michael," urged his mother, "you listen to your papa. You cannot join this war. Your duty is here. This war is none of our business. Besides, with the new land to clear and all the work with our hired hand gone, we need you here on the farm. Tell him, Papa."

Mike put down his fork and faced his mother. "First, Momma, I want to apologize for my actions in town today. I had no right to do what I did. I acted without thinking of the embarrassment or the consequences for the family. Susan tried her best to stop me, but I didn't listen to her. Instead, I allowed my anger to cloud my judgment.

"But, Momma, when this war began over a year ago, I stayed on the farm as you asked. Everyone thought it would be over after a short time, anyway. But it didn't end. And now, our president has asked for more volunteers for the Army. He is trying to keep our country together. I can't stay home any longer while others, my schoolmates and neighbors, go off to fight and die for our country. Even that worthless son of the banker has joined. How can I live here and not be considered a coward? No, Momma, I know I have a duty to my family. But I have a duty to our country, too. It is time I satisfied that responsibility.

"I hope you understand, Papa," Mike said quietly but without hesitation. "It is time for me to join this fight. So, I want to tell the Justice of the Peace that I accept my guilt for assaulting Bacon. I hope you will not try to pay the fine.

Instead, allow me to take the option he gave me of joining that cavalry regiment being formed in Grand Rapids."

Everyone sat quietly, waiting for Jake's reply.

"So, Momma," he said, "it is decided. Now, finish your dinner, everyone. We all have chores to finish today."

Everyone was very quiet the rest of the day. They sat together eating supper with hardly a word exchanged. After dark that evening, Susan wrote of it in her diary.

***

Dear Diary,

You will not believe what happened today. Michael got into a fight in town. Well, it wasn't much of a fight, actually. He lost his temper when our old schoolmate Carl Bacon called him a coward for not joining the Army. He dumped Carl into a water trough. I tried to stop him. But when Michael gets his temper up, there is no holding him. The result was that Michael got arrested for assault. Was Papa mad? I've never seen him so angry.

But the most surprising thing is that when we were telling the rest of the family about it at dinner time, Michael announced that he was joining the Army instead of allowing my parents to pay a fine for his breaking the law. I couldn't believe he spoke to our parents that way.

Papa agreed to let him join. I suppose the fact that Michael is eighteen and could join without permission may have had something to do with it.

After the boys and Papa left for the barn, Momma cried. I've never seen her cry before, but she did. Ann and I did, too, a little.

Later at supper, no one said a word the whole time. I guess nothing seemed important enough after what had happened earlier in the day. More later — Susan

***

It was Sunday morning. As usual, the Drieborg family was at St. Robert's Catholic Church for the ten o'clock Mass. The two girls and their mother wore their best summer dresses. The two boys and their father wore white shirts and ties under their black wool suit jackets.

A head covering was mandatory for ladies attending a Catholic Church service. The Drieborg girls and their mother chose to wear white lace caps pinned to their hair. The custom for men was quite the opposite. They were to uncover their heads when entering a Catholic Church.

Father Farrell delivered a sermon in which he stressed controlling one's temper. *"He's looking right at me,"* Mike thought. The priest probably knew of the scrape Mike had gotten into the day before with Carl Bacon. In a small town like Lowell, everyone would have known by now.

The priest also led his parish in prayer for those in the Army. "Lord, look after our boys who are defending our freedoms and our Union. Amen." Mike squirmed in his pew. *"I'll be darned. Father Farrell is looking right at me again."* There were very few young men Mike's age in attendance. Most of them were in the Army, except Mike. He felt the stares.

Attending Sunday services was important to Lowell area families. Few missed what they regarded as their Sunday obligation, and few wanted to miss the opportunity to socialize. With homes widely scattered throughout the area, there was infrequent contact during the week. So, after the Sunday service, most churchgoers gathered for a potluck meal.

Those at St. Robert's were no exception. After Mass was concluded, the families in attendance gathered for a meal. Because of the summer weather, they set up tables and benches in a tree-shaded area next to the church. The women went to their wagons and got the plates and bowls of food they brought from home for sharing.

Once everyone had their fill, the dinnerware was washed, and the tables cleared. The men stood around in the shade of the trees, smoking pipes and talking about farming and the war.

With so many of the young men in the Union army, the conversation had become strained lately. After all, some of the boys had been wounded, others killed. So, on these occasions, Jake was usually quiet. But he couldn't help but think to himself,

"What do I say? Dick Norman's boy was killed at Bull Run. George Kielhoffer's son Bill was wounded in June, I think. Da Havilands haven't heard anything about der boy David since he left last May. Dave Hauenstein has two boys serving somewhere.

"Da other boys, I get da names all mixed up. Da men have often looked at me sort of like dey want to know why Michael is not in da Army, like der sons."

The women sat around the tables and talked, too. They shared recipes and garden news. They all knew whose boy had been killed, wounded, or missing. Everyone in the village knew these things. They also knew that Rose Drieborg's son Michael was still at home, safe.

Even so, when Rose was present, they were all very careful not to ask why Michael wasn't serving in the Army like their own sons. So, it had been a bit strained on these Sundays after church. Everyone sort of tiptoed around. No one said what was really on her mind.

Rose was quiet this Sunday after church, too. She knew the word would be out soon about Michael being forced to join the Army.

"I wonder how each of my friends will take such news? Those with sons of their own in the Army will probably think, 'It's about time for that Drieborg boy to enlist.' Others might be harsher and think, 'It took the Justice of the Peace to tell him, join up or go to jail.'

"I would gladly suffer their scorn to keep Michael home and away from war."

***

Michael was taking a break from the baseball game.

"Hey, Mike!" one of Mike's friends called out. "I hear you got into another scrape with Carl. Didn't know he was back in town. I thought he was still at the university."

"He was there, Billy," Mike responded, "but they threw him out. After that, his father bought him a commission in the Union Army. And, yes, he and I did have a fight. Not much of one, though. I just dunked him in the horse trough for beating on a little kid with his riding crop."

"That's pretty much what I heard. Did you get arrested for that?"

"You might as well hear it from me. You heard right. Carl's dad filed charges, and Marshal Chapman had to arrest me. No other way to say it."

"Why aren't you in jail, then?" asked Billy. "I thought when a person's arrested, they're in jail."

"I don't know much about those things either," Mike responded. "I guess I thought the same thing. But, the Justice of the Peace gave me a choice. Serve thirty days in the Grand Rapids jail, pay a fine of one hundred dollars, or join the cavalry regiment over in Grand Rapids."

"What are you gonna do, Mike?"

"We talked about it at home yesterday. My folks wanted to pay the fine. But I decided that I would volunteer for the Army. Like you, when the war broke out last year, I obeyed my parents and stayed home. I was underage anyway, and the Army wouldn't let me volunteer without my father's approval.

"When he refused his permission, I had little choice but to stay home.

"Things are different now. Since I turned eighteen in May, I can volunteer without his permission. And with the war dragging on as it has, I think it's time I answered Mr. Lincoln's call for volunteers and help keep our country together. That's what I've decided to do."

"I wish my parents would let me join up, Mike," Billy complained. "But I suppose I'll have to wait until next year when I turn eighteen. Anyway, good luck to you."

"Thanks, Billy."

Leaving the Farm

Even though it was still dark outside, Mike was awake. He just lay there in bed, looking up at the roof beams. For many years, his internal clock had awakened him a few minutes before he heard his father in the kitchen, starting the morning fire in his mother's Dutch oven. Once he got it going, she would begin her breakfast preparations. By the time chores were done, she would have fresh bread and a big breakfast ready. That was his favorite meal of the day.

This day was different, though. He couldn't remember a night when he had slept less. After all, this was the day he intended to plead guilty to a serious crime. He had assaulted someone.

He wondered, *"Will the Army people know what I did? That I chose to join over going to jail?*

The thought kept coming back to him — *"Now that I'm a criminal, will they trust me?"*

At one point during the long night, Mike thought, *"Maybe my decision to volunteer was a mistake. Maybe I should let Papa pay the fine and stay home until after the harvest, as he and I had agreed. Then I could volunteer. The Army people would never know, would they? Momma would like that, too".*

He rolled over and punched his pillow again. Little Jake was snoring softly, safely asleep beside him.

"No!" he thought. *"That's not right. In the first place, where would my parents get one hundred dollars? And then to have me skip out and volunteer in three months or so would be cruel of me. How could I use them that way?*

"What's the matter with me all of a sudden? I assaulted someone in town, on a Saturday, no less, just because he made me angry. That was bad enough. But it was not just 'someone.' No, it had to be the son of the only banker in Lowell.

"This is the same banker who Papa needs for loans to finance the farm operation from time to time, the same banker who holds the mortgage on my parents' farm. He

is known to have denied loans to people he didn't like and ruined people who angered him. My reckless behavior put my parents in danger of both."

Mike's papa appeared at the top of the ladder to the loft. "Michael," he whispered, "come now, da chores."

Mike swung his legs out of bed, stretched, and rubbed his eyes. In a few minutes, he was by the back door, pulling on his boots. There was a morning chill, so he put on his wool jacket, too.

"Michael," his momma whispered, "here, eat this biscuit."

He took a good-sized bite. It was left over from last night's supper. But his mother had warmed it and had put a big scoop of butter and strawberry preserves on it just for him.

"Umm," he mumbled. "Thanks, Momma."

He stuffed the rest of the biscuit into his mouth and joined his father in the barn to begin milking their two cows. All told, the two men had about an hour of early chores. Once he had swallowed the last of his momma's treat, he wanted to talk with his father.

"If the word I have is correct, Papa," Mike began, "the cavalry regiment I'm joining in Grand Rapids will not be formed until late August or early September. That should give us time to clear a few more acres of the river land and get the new sheep flock settled. Don't you think?"

There was a separate wooden stall for each of the two cows in the Drieborg barn. Each man sat in one of these stalls on a low three-legged stool while he milked a cow. In the silence, Mike heard the barn animal sounds, the chickens in the yard, and the hissing sound of the squirted warm milk hitting the bucket. He did not hear his father reply to his question, just silence.

Mike remained silent as well.

Shortly, his father walked by Mike's stall to empty his full bucket of milk into a milk separator. "Ya, Michael, der is plenty of time for dose things. We see, eh? For now, we finish da chores. Momma has breakfast for us early, so we are not late for your trial. Dis morning, at least one of da Drieborg men will be a man of good character. He will be on time. Come now, Michael, we have chores to finish."

"Ouch! That hurt," Mike thought.

The two men finished quickly and washed up for breakfast. As usual, it was a hearty meal. Mike's momma served biscuits and gravy and fried bacon with fried potatoes and eggs.

"Michael," Rose said, "put on your Sunday suit, white shirt, and tie. I won't have you in Mr. Deeb's courtroom looking like a farmhand."

Mike just nodded his head and headed for the loft to change his clothes.

Then she turned to her husband. "You too, Jake Drieborg." But he was already behind the closed door of their bedroom, changing.

Jake drove the wagon into Lowell. According to his watch, it wasn't yet eight o 'clock. In fact, they still had fifteen minutes before the court would be open.

Mike turned to his father. "Papa, I am so sorry that I let my temper cloud my judgment Saturday. I would give anything if I could take it all back. I wish that it had never happened. I know I embarrassed the family, let you down, and exposed you to Mr. Bacon's anger. I hope you and Momma can forgive me."

Jake just sat on the wagon's bench seat hunched forward, listening to his son speak. He still held the reins in his hands.

"Please say something, Papa," Mike silently shouted.

Jake finally did. "Michael," he said, still not looking at his son. "Neider Momma or I could ever believe you would do such a thing. We never thought you would act like a bully. Yes, you let us down. But you are my son, and you are going away soon. Maybe I never see you again, with dis war you are going to fight. We have no time for anger, you and me, I think. So, I forgive dis mistake you have made."

Now, Jake looked directly at his son.

"Parents, especially da momma, love der children, no matter what. But children must earn da trust, especially from da papa. Now listen, Michael. You have my forgiveness, and you will always have my love. But you have lost my trust."

Mike slumped against the back of the wagon's bench seat. The air seemed to have been punched out of him. His hands clutched the seat. He broke eye contact with his father.

Jake went on. "I want you to promise me that you will do everything you can to earn back my trust. Will you do dat, Michael?"

Mike looked at his father. "Yes, Papa, I promise."

"And," Jake went on, "will you promise me dat whatever you do in dis army you are joining will make me and Momma proud? Ya?"

"Yes, Papa," Mike replied, still shaken by his father's words, "I promise."

Jake had never hugged either of his sons, but he put his hand on Mike's shoulder and gave it a light squeeze. "Good. Now, it is time for da court."

Mike and his father entered the building and took the same seats they had used Saturday, in front of Mr. Deeb's desk.

"Good morning," Mr. Deeb said.

He wore a long black robe this time, Mike observed. Seated across from the Drieborgs, he called his court to order and read aloud the complaint brought against Michael Drieborg for assaulting Carl Bacon.

"What have you decided, Jake?"

Mike's father straightened up in his chair. "Dis was a big decision for da family. Since Michael is da person who will have to live with it, I'll let him tell you."

Mr. Deeb looked directly at Mike. "Well, Michael?"

"It was decided, sir..." he responded, "it was decided that I would join the cavalry unit being formed in Grand Rapids, sir."

"Fine; that then will be the ruling of this court," Mr. Deeb pronounced. As soon as he filled out the paperwork, he turned to Michael again. "You are to sign here. By so signing, you are pleading guilty to the charge of assault. Further, you choose to enlist in the Union Army instead of spending thirty days in the county jail at Grand Rapids or paying a fine of one hundred dollars."

"Yes, Sir," Mike responded. "Will that stay on my record forever?"

"No, son. In fact, one year from today, as long as you are still serving in the Union Army, or upon your death or an honorable discharge, it will be stricken from your record. I also prepared this other document, whereby you agree to volunteer in the Sixth Cavalry Regiment. By signing, you agree to report to their training area in Grand Rapids on the first Sunday of September before five in the afternoon. Do you understand?"

"Yes, sir, we do," Jake answered.

"Michael?"

"Yes, sir, I understand, too." Mike signed both documents.

"This court stands adjourned."

They all rose and shook hands. Thirty minutes after having arrived in Lowell, they left.

***

Several weeks later, Jake and his two sons were finishing the morning chores on a Sunday morning.

"Come, boys," Jake told them. "Momma will be angry if her breakfast gets cold, waiting for us."

As they entered the house, the three male Drieborgs could smell the freshly baked bread and fried bacon waiting for them on the dining room table.

"Well, Jacob," Rose announced, "another few minutes, and the food would be cold. Were the animals cranky this morning, or were you just slow today?"

Jake reacted to Rose's frosty greeting lightly. "See boys, why I told you we must hurry with da chores? Good thing da food is not cold."

Without further comment, Rose took her accustomed seat at the table. Jake said the prayer, and Rose began to pass the plates of food. After finishing, they would all go to church in Lowell, as was their custom on a Sunday morning.

But this was not the usual Sunday. Today, Rose's eldest child Michael was leaving home. He had agreed to report for training this day as a soldier in the Union Army, eventually to fight and possibly die in the War of Rebellion now raging.

Mike thought it was unusually quiet at the breakfast table this morning. He didn't know how to act or talk. He knew that his parents, his mother in particular, did not want him to leave. So he remained silent. His brother and sisters were also silent, not knowing what to say either. His father remained impassive. His mother picked at her food. He could see that she was close to tears.

Toward the end of the meal, she broke the silence. "Papa," she said, "I want to go with you when you take Michael to the training camp."

"No, Momma," Jake announced. "You and I have talked of dis already. After da service and we eat dinner at da church, I will drop you and da girls off here at home. Little Jake and I will take Michael to da camp in Grand Rapids. You will stay here with da girls."

"But, Papa!" she pleaded.

"No more talk, Momma," Jake insisted, softening the tone of his voice. "Michael will say his goodbye to you and his sisters here at home, not in front of hundreds of men.

"Besides, the roads might not be safe. Der will be hundreds of men going to dat camp in Grand Rapids today. And there will be many others returning to der homes after taking men to da same camp. It might not be good dat you, a woman, be traveling on da road today.

"Come, now we must clean up and leave for church. Da Drieborgs are not late for Sunday Mass, eh Momma?"

***

At church, the women of the Drieborg family usually sang with great enthusiasm, but not today. They just couldn't get over the fact that Michael was leaving for the army that afternoon. The other women of the church understood their feelings since most of them had gone through the same thing.

Later that afternoon, Jake dropped off the women at home despite their tears and pleading.

"Say your goodbye to Michael here, Momma."

Mike hugged his sisters and promised his mother that he would be careful. The parting was full of tears, even for him. So, he took the Bible his mother had given him and left the house quickly to join his father and brother on the wagon. Then they headed to Grand Rapids and the training camp.

Back at home, Rose gathered herself. "All right, girls, enough of the crying. Get your garden clothing on. We have work to do."

Later that afternoon, the girls had washed up and were taking a rest. Ann sat on her bed with her diary.

***

Dear Diary,

Well, Michael is gone. Now I know how my girlfriends felt when their brothers enlisted. This war wasn't supposed to last this long. So many of our school friends have had family members die or be badly hurt. I haven't heard any news from Ethan for months. For all I know, he is dead, just like Willie. Oh, how I hate this awful war. More later. Ann

***

The three Drieborg men traveled west on Fulton Street. Heavy woods lined both sides of the road. Every now and then, a clearing would appear, revealing a farmhouse, a barn, and sometimes other small buildings.

"Not much different from our layout, is it, Papa?" Jacob suggested.

More than once, Jake slowed the wagon and surveyed the situation. Once, he disagreed with his younger son.

"Dey haven't cleared enough land for crops, son. Dey will have a hard time paying their bank loan on dat place until dey do."

Mike had traveled this far from home when the family had come to hear Mr. Lincoln speak back in the fall of 1860. He still found the changing landscape fascinating. As they neared the city, the road seemed wider and more worn than it was near their Lowell home.

He knew that Fulton Street would not take them directly to the camp. So, as they neared the city limits, they looked for a road running north called Prospect Street.

"There it is, Papa," Mike pointed out. "That street sign says Prospect Street. It's up that hill to our right."

His father pulled up. They sat in the wagon, allowing the horse to rest before heading up the steep hill.

Before they turned onto Fountain Street, they had a clear view of the city. "My goodness, Papa," Little Jake exclaimed, "we can see the whole town from here."

And they could. The city was located on both sides of a wide river. The hills on each side made it look as though Grand Rapids was in a bowl.

"Look at the boats on the river," Mike observed, "and see all the tall buildings? Sure is a lot bigger than Lowell."

"It appears so," his father said. "But I would not want to live in such a crowded place. Lowell is better for us, I think."

Jake alerted the horse with a snap of the reins, and it began to turn and pull the wagon to the right, up the steep incline of Prospect Street. It didn't take long to reach the next cross street, called Fountain Street. They had been told that the training camp would be one hundred yards or so to the east of that crossroads.

The entire area was crowded, like downtown Lowell on a Saturday morning. Dozens of horse-drawn wagons were coming and going near the camp entrance. Families were milling about or picnicking in nearby fields.

Jake spoke to his younger son. "Jacob, I don't want you telling your sisters or your momma about all da families we see here today. Da women are upset enough. Do you understand me, son?"

"Yes, Papa."

Mike pointed to an opening, and his father directed the wagon off the road.

"Give me those two packages, little brother," Mike said.

Little Jake handed him the small bundle of clothing. His mother had insisted he take several changes of underwear. The second package contained cookies, fresh bread, and slices of ham and cheese.

"You never know how long it will be until they feed you, Michael," she had warned him.

Mike gave his brother a big hug. "You take care, Jacob," he urged him." I'm sure you'll do fine without me around. Remember, you have to look after our sisters now."

"You know I will, Michael."

Jake interrupted. "Stay with da wagon, Jacob. I'll be right back. Come, Michael. Walk with me a bit."

As they walked side by side, Mike felt his father's hand on his shoulder. When they stopped near the entrance to the camp, they could see men hurrying everywhere.

Jake turned to his son. He still had his right hand on Mike's shoulder. "It will be almost dark when we reach home, son. And you must report in. So, we must go.

"I wish you were not going to fight in dis war. But you have given your word. Remember, Michael, our talk about controlling your temper. Stay away from dat no-good Bacon boy. He will cause trouble for you if he can."

"Yes, Papa," Mike responded.

Jake's grip tightened on his son's shoulder. "You must do your duty, son. And you must always behave with honor."

"I promise, Papa," Mike responded. "I will do my duty and bring honor to the Drieborg name."

Jake embraced his son, turned, and walked away.

Mike watched his father walk away and thought, *"That's the first time I've ever seen tears in my father's eyes."*

As the wagon pulled away toward home, Mike said aloud: "Don't worry, Papa. I won't disappoint you. I'll do my duty."

Afterword

Mike walked through the camp gate under a sign which read *Camp Kellogg*. Another sign below read: '*Home of the 6th Michigan Cavalry Regiment.*'

After standing in lines for two hours, Mike left the commissary building with clothing and gear piled high on his arms.

Mike asked a recruit standing behind him, "What troop are you assigned to?"

"They told me to find the I Troop barracks," the other man responded.

"I was told that, too," Mike said. "Let's ask that man leaning against that building over there. He looks important enough to know what's going on."

Mike and the other recruit walked over to the man.

"Sir," Mike said, "we've been assigned to I Troop. Do we go into this building?"

"I'm not a sir, Private," he snapped. "I'm First Sergeant Williams of I Troop. Who might you be?"

"Michael Drieborg, First Sergeant."

"So, you're Drieborg," observed Williams. As he said this, he stood erect to his six-foot-two height, hands on his hips. He leaned forward and looked Mike in the eyes. "I'll be having a serious talk with you real soon, Private. For now, go inside this barrack," he ordered. "Report to Sergeant Riley. He's looking forward to seeing you too, Drieborg."

Mike and the other recruit moved past the first sergeant and into the building.

"You know that guy?" Mike's companion asked.

"I never met the man."

"The way he looked at you, I'd hate to be in your shoes."

"*Holy crap!*" Mike thought. "*Isn't it enough that I've got Bacon to watch out for? Why do I have First Sergeant Williams to worry about, too?*"

As Michael Drieborg began his life as a soldier in the Union Army, he was sure he would soon find out.

Sources

Lincoln for President: An Unlikely Candidate: An Audacious Strategy: And the Victory No One Saw Coming. Bruce Chadwick. Sourcebooks Inc. Naperville Illinois, 2009.

Lincoln and the Election of 1860. Michael S. Green. Southern University Press. Carbondale, Illinois, 2011.

Tariffs, Blockades, and Inflation: The Economics of the Civil War. Mark Thornton and Robert B. Ekelund, Jr. Scholarly Resources Inc. Wilmington, DE, 2004.

America: The Last Best Hope. Vol. I. William J. Bennett. Nelson Current, Nashville, Tennessee, 2006.

About the Author

Michael J. Deeb was born and raised in Grand Rapids, Michigan. His undergraduate and graduate education centered on American studies. His doctorate was in management. He was an educator for nineteen years, most of which saw him teaching American history.

His personal life found him as a pre-teen spending time regularly at the public library, reading non-fiction works of history. This passion has continued to this day. Teaching at the college, university, and high school levels only increased his love for such reading and research.

Since 2005, he and his wife, Sally Dittman, have lived in Sun City Center, FL. In the fall of 2007, he finished the Civil War-era historical novel *Duty and Honor*. The sequel, *Duty Accomplished*, was completed in 2008. *Honor Restored* was made available in 2009. *The Lincoln Assassination* was published in 2011.

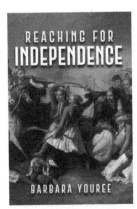

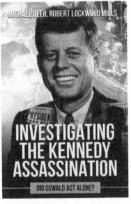

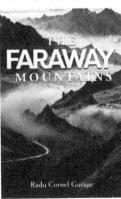